# CONSTABLE GARRETT

## AND THE DEAD RINGER

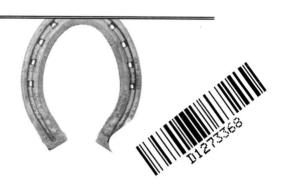

## Don Gutteridge

Constable Garrett and the Dead Ringer
Copyright © 2016 by Don Gutteridge

Tellwell Talent
www.tellwell.ca

ISBN
978-1-77302-196-6 (Paperback)
978-1-77302-197-3 (eBook)

# CHAPTER 1

The CNR Express screeched to a halt in front of the Petroleum City train station. But the bustling oil town was not the destination of Stan Garrett, who stepped eagerly onto the platform, hatless, and without baggage. And that was the way he wanted it, hoped that it would be if all went well in the interview.

"Is there a bus to Port Eddy?" he asked the porter after he had finished helping an elderly woman with her luggage.

"You just missed it, sir. But the village centre is less than a mile from here. You could walk it in twenty minutes. Or take that taxicab over there."

Garrett thanked the man and glanced at his watch. He had plenty of time, and if this unknown village was to become his home for the foreseeable future, then a walk-through would serve some purpose besides taking him to the meeting-place.

"Which way, then?" he asked.

The porter turned back, still smiling his indelible smile. "That way. Due north along Water Street. When you cross Petroleum Drive you'll be in the village." He upgraded his smile to a grin. "But don't blink or you may miss it."

Water Street turned out to be one of the City's main thoroughfares, crammed with shops whose display windows shone brightly in the warm sunshine of an early September day in the year 1932. Garrett paid them little heed. All his thoughts were on the task ahead, though it proved impossible for him not to review, however fleetingly, the events in his life that had brought him here to be vetted by the village council for the position of town constable – indeed the only constable in a municipality of six hundred and fifty souls (a figure that may have included several dogs and coven or two of cats).

He had told no-one of his journey from the province's largest city to one of its tinier villages, not even his parents or his closest friends. If nothing came of it, then no-one but he himself would be the wiser. If he were offered the job, then there would be time enough for explanations and goodbyes. He doubted that any of his associates on the Toronto Police Force would be too surprised by such a sudden – and on the face of it – inexplicable move. For even though he had been a patrolman with a meritorious record and eight years of service and, indeed, had applied for and been accepted as a detective constable in the plainclothes division, the heart had gone out of his work. And, he admitted daily, he had done little to hide the fact. The sudden death of his wife from an aneurysm two years ago had left him devastated. The application for detective status, a move he had only vaguely considered before Anna's vanishing, was, he knew now, a desperate attempt to renew his interest in living, in moving resolutely into the future rather than drifting with its fickle currents.

The shops on Water Street petered out, and now there appeared a salt works, a major dairy with its sprawling horse-barns, and numerous small factories and commercial businesses. The river to his left was not visible, but he could hear the peremptory blast of two lake-steamers passing one another. Ahead he could see another major street, Petroleum Drive, beyond which he would find the village itself. He knew nothing about it except its size and geographical location – at the junction of the Great Lake and the river into which it poured its blue fury. The advertisement for the position of village constable had been posted in his locker room at Third Division with just the barest of details, not the least of which was a monthly salary of fifty dollars and the promise of house to be occupied rent-free. Garrett had applied, and received a positive reply by return mail. He guessed that there had not been too many applicants.

He reached Petroleum Drive, loud with automobiles and panel-trucks to-ing and fro-ing along the road that, he could see, ended at the entrance to an imposing grain elevator. Across the street, however, there was no sign of a village. Rather, he faced a park to his left and a smoking foundry of some sort to his right. However, a roadway that appeared to wind through the park connected with Water Street, and surely would debouch into the village proper on the far side.

It was a pleasant park, tall-treed and still leafy with a late-summer breeze. No car passed him either way. At this moment he relished the solitude, where the pull of the past and the draw of the future seemed momentarily irrelevant. It didn't last. Anna was always somewhere in his thoughts, and her abrupt departure was certainly in its way the reason he found himself almost two hundred miles from the place that had been his home since he was twelve years old. They had tried for children, only to have Anna suffer two miscarriages and a stillbirth. All that stress and strain had been too much for her perhaps. Her death had been quick and painless, his life lonely and pain-wracked. Little wonder that the profession he had chosen as a young man failed to fascinate thereafter. Still, some urge without a name had moved him to apply for detective status. He had passed an exam. He had survived an interview.

Today's interview would seem like child's play. And perhaps that was what he was seeking – a simpler life, one where he might pretend to make a fresh start, even though he knew there was no such thing. A life lived could not be unlived. But his childhood, despite his having no brothers or sisters, had been a happy one, and that happiness now glowed more brightly as he looked back on it. The place near Toronto where he had been raised was a sleepy farm village that had been enlivened by the fantasies of its youngsters – his neighbours and his boyhood pals. The plainer the setting, the more vivid and necessary the imagination. Cops and robbers had been the staple game. He had been a cop – always.

Garret stepped out of the park and onto the street that would lead him into the heart of Port Eddy. There were now plain, clapboard houses on either side – a rusting sign telling him he was on King Street. He passed several people and was surprised that they neither nodded a greeting nor paid him the slightest attention. This was no dozing country village where everyone entering its precincts was either known or not – familiar or stranger – and treated as such. Then he remembered that this was a port town, despite its modest size. A few hundred yards west of King Street there would be dockyards and freight-sheds along the river's shoreline. And feeding it the CNR spur line that, according to his map, looped around the village like a stiff necklace. There would be noise and commotion here, the bustle of business. And strangers from the docked ships: sailors, sea-captains, ste-vedores. Still, King Street was quiet enough for four o'clock on a Friday afternoon. He passed three ordinary intersect-ing streets – Princess, Viscount and Elizabeth – and paused when he came to what was evidently the centre of town. For, on the corner of King and Edward Streets, he spotted a con-fectionary store with a gas-pump outside of it, a dairy-bar to his right, and catty-corner to him a fire hall – the latter closed up and soundless. He found himself thirsty, and as he was twenty minutes early for his appointment, he decided to treat himself to a milkshake.

The dairy-bar – whistle-clean and fresh-smelling – was empty, but he had just sat himself down on a stool at the counter when the proprietor emerged from a doorway, a wide smile on her face.

"Hello," she said cheerily. "What'll you have?"

Garrett ordered a chocolate milkshake.

"Coming right up." She turned to the bay of ice-cream bins and flavour-spouts, and began preparing his shake. She was not what Garrett imagined an ice-cream jockey, even in a small village, should look like. She was just under middle age with the bearing of a woman of breeding and a tailored suit to match. The apron that protected it from ice-cream spills was appliquéd in some abstract manner that reminded Garrett of the strange paintings he had once seen in the Art Gallery of Ontario. Her auburn hair was tucked up in a roll and pinned with two simple silver clasps. She spoke to him with her back turned.

"You off the boat, then?" she said, puzzled.

"Not really. I've just come from the Toronto train."

"That would be the Express. I'm not surprised. Unless you were a steward or an officer, I wouldn't have picked you out as having arrived by water."

"You get a lot of visitors from the ships that dock here." It was more a statement than a question.

"I'd be out of business otherwise. I serve a good cup of coffee, and the word spreads."

"There is no restaurant in town?"

"Used to be, but the food was so bad even the sailor-boys wouldn't eat it."

"You're it, then?"

She poured the contents of the well-shaken shake into a frosted glass and turned to serve it to him. "There's a confectioner, a baker and a grocer – if you wish three courses of dessert or are of a mind to cook your own."

She thrust out her hand, letting her keen, intelligent eyes rest on Garrett in his best suit and his only silk tie. "I'm Maud Marsden by the way. I own this place."

"Stan Garrett."

They shook hands, her grasp as firm as any man's.

"But that's the name of the gentleman we're interviewing for Franny Piersall's job."

"That's why I'm here," Garrett said with a satisfying pull on two straws.

"Well, then, welcome to Port Eddy, young man."

"Thank you. Perhaps you wouldn't mind telling me about the job I'm applying for. I've only read the advertisement that went out to all police departments."

Maud Marsden gave him a quizzical smile and said, "I'd be glad to."

"What happened to the man who was your constable? Franny, ah – "

"Piersall." She sighed. "Passed away. Massive stroke. Two weeks ago."

"Two weeks ago?"

"I know it seems unseemly, doesn't it, but the council feel we can't be without a policeman for too long before the cutthroats and homicidal maniacs overrun us. Besides, nobody in town relished the thought of being policed in the interim by the City cops."

"But you're not that worried?" Garrett grinned, warming quickly to this woman and glad that he had decided to stop here for refreshment.

"Well, the only crime wave we've had recently is a rash of stolen bicycles."

"Bicycles?"

"Whisked away mysteriously, only to show up in one field or another with a spoke or two out of place. And, by the bye, a rash is a total of three incidents."

Garret imbibed more of his milkshake. "So you're wondering what a person like me would want with a job that sounds as if boredom might be the most attractive feature?"

"Am I that transparent?" Maud said with a small frown. Then she brightened and added, "Either that or you've got the makings of a good detective."

Garrett's surprise showed.

"Oh, there aren't many secrets in this burg. None, in fact. It's widely known that you are an experienced policeman from Toronto who had ambitions to be a detective."

Had his resumé been circulated everywhere in town? He was glad he had kept it short and to the point.

"I was born and raised in a small place," he felt constrained to say. "I've decided to make a major career change before it's too late."

"Tired of big-city life?"

"Something like that."

"What does your wife think of such a move?" She was staring at his wedding ring.

"She passed away two years ago," he said solemnly. "I'm on my own."

Genuine sympathy registered on Maud's face immediately – and something else perhaps. Perhaps a re-evaluation of sorts? "I'm sorry to hear that. I'm a widow myself, but Harold died fifteen years ago. I hardly think of myself in that way any more. But I can see now why you might wish to pull up stakes and try something new."

"Thank you for your concern."

"Still, this is a pretty quiet place. Your professional skills may well be underused, should you be offered the job. Certainly there's been no need for detective work since the freight office was held up five years ago. Our Franny Piersall was more like an avuncular figure about town than a policeman. We've known no other. He was here for forty years or more."

"I see," Garrett said, finishing his milkshake and beginning to have some doubts about the wisdom of coming here. Well, he didn't have to accept the position even if it were offered. The pay was minimal, even with the rent-free house.

Maud appeared to be reading his thoughts. "It's a very pleasant little cottage he lived in. The village owns it, but Franny was there so long we all accepted that it was his place. He was a bachelor, by the way, and he's left all the furniture and doo-dads where they were. He had no heirs to claim his personal belongings. The successful candidate will be allowed to move right in."

"That would be very convenient for me."

"I'd ask the reeve, who'll be chairing the interview, for an inspection of the premises."

Garrett dropped fifteen cents on the counter. "I'm just surprised your council wouldn't want to save fifty dollars a month by letting the province take care of policing, and perhaps rent the constable's house to someone else. After all, this depression is now almost three years old and looking to get worse."

"A perceptive point, Mr. Garrett," she said with an approving smile, "but if we gave up our policeman, we'd have to become a police village with the danger of succumbing to the annexationist dreams of Petroleum City. Either option would mean sacrificing our independence. There is nothing more sacred to the citizens here than their independence. It'll take a lot more poverty and deprivation to bring us to the brink of capitulation. You may be considering a career move to a quiet village, young man, but it's not a dormant one."

"You make it sound almost exciting."

She smiled. "Well now, I wouldn't go that far."

Garrett looked at his watch. "I've five minutes to go," he said. "I assume that odd-looking building over there is the library where the meeting will take place – as it's next to the fire hall."

"Your powers of deduction are acute," Maud said, undoing her apron strings.

"I'll be off, then. Thanks very much for chatting. And the great milkshake."

"Don't be in such a hurry, Mr. Garrett. I've just got to lock up the shop behind me, and then we'll walk over there together."

"I don't understand – "

"I not only run this dairy-bar, young man. I am one of the village councillors."

Garrett and Maud Marsden walked across the street and past the fire hall towards a squat storey-and-a-half brick building with a wide set of plank stairs leading up to the double doors of what had to be the village library. On the window of the sunken lower floor Garrett thought he caught a glimpse of bars.

Maud noted his surprised expression and said, "Yes, those are bars. We keep our felons down there, close to the uplifting literature directly above the cells."

"And the library serves you as a town hall?"

"It's all we got to show for fifty years of incorporation."

"And the cells are often occupied?"

"The only one to grace them in recent months has been Alvin Hodge, who prefers to sleep off his drunk there than to go home and face his missus."

Garrett smiled, though he was starting to wonder if Port Eddy really needed an officer of the law.

"Here we are, then," Maud said, pulling open a door heavy enough to have served the cells below.

Breezy Harker, the reeve (who moonlighted as the town barber) called the meeting to order by rapping his knuckles on the polished library table, around which his secretary and three councillors had arranged themselves. Garrett was seated at the far end opposite him, and had a clear view of the man. He looked to be in his mid-forties, so slim and wiry he could have been cast as Shakespeare's Cassius, should there ever be established a local theatre troupe. His dark hair was combed back and slicked down with one of his shop's many unguents, and his cheeks were shaved so close they appeared to have been buffed.

"This special meeting of the council is now officially in session," Breezy boomed in a voice orotund enough to have reached the back rows of an opera-house. The thin, spare

woman with the poised pencil winced at the pronounce-
ment and glanced longingly aside where she was surrounded
by the comfort of books who spoke only when asked to.

"Welcome to Port Eddy," said Farley Joiner, grocer and
rookie councillor.

Breezy glanced sharply at Joiner and said, "Yes, a warm
Port Eddy welcome to you, Constable Stan Garrett. Let me
introduce you to my fellow council members. Miss Marsden
I see you have already met." He gave Maud a look that suggested she had committed some breech of protocol by way-
laying their guest.

"Ma'am," Garrett said with a polite nod.

"And these are Max Barwise on my left, who operates the
billiard parlour farther up the street, and Farley Joiner, our
grocer, on my right."

"You didn't wear your uniform," Joiner said, and got a
glare from the chairman.

"I consider myself off-duty," Garrett said with a glance at
Maud, who was trying not to smile too broadly.

"Just so," Breezy said. "And you'll find that, however you
may run meetings such as this in the capital city, we here in
Port Eddy like to keep matters informal."

"What Mr. Harker means to say," Max Barwise said to
Garrett, "is we've never had an interview for a policeman's
job before."

This time it was Garrett who had to suppress a smile.
Barwise looked at him with an expression that bespoke intelligence and a vast sympathy for the foibles of his fellows.
Garrett noticed that the sleeve of his left arm drooped life-
lessly at his side. Barwise was one-armed.

Joiner spotted Garrett's response and said, "Max lost his arm at Vimy Ridge." Joiner was a small man of middle years who looked as if the weight of the world was glued to his shoulders. His sharp features exaggerated the hollows and creases in his flesh. Garrett had the impression of a defrocked bantam rooster.

"I'm sure our guest is not interested in our life stories," Breezy Harker said abruptly. "If so, he'd be here well past dark."

"You've forgotten Hannah," Joiner said.

"My apologies," Breezy said with no real contrition. "This is our council secretary and part-time librarian, Miss Hannah Bristol."

The person in question was one who seemed born to be overlooked. She was as thin as a rail with tiny angular features, braided brown locks, and an expression that suggested perpetual surprise. She flushed at the mention of her name.

"But everybody in town calls her Miss Hannah," Max Barwise said gently.

"Enough of introductions, then," Breezy said. "Let's get right down to business. Constable Garrett has come a long way today."

There was an uncomfortable pause. Miss Hannah's pencil could be heard skidding to a stop.

"Why don't we let the constable tell us why he wishes the position," Maud said, turning to Garrett.

The chairman said nothing, but his stare spoke volumes. He glowered at Maud Marsden in a way that made it clear he considered her presence in this male domain an unforgivable affront to decorum and decency. For Maud had not only refused to sell the dairy-bar her father had willed to her, she had had the temerity to take on the proprietorship and operate the business more successfully than her parent had. And to top off this series of indignities, she had run for village council and won election handily. To rub salt in the wound, she never missed a single meeting, even if it meant closing her shop early.

"Please, proceed, sir," Breezy said as if he himself had thought of Maud's suggestion.

Garrett cleared his throat and began. "Basically I'm looking for a career move. As you know from my resumé, I was a patrolman for eight years on the Toronto Police Force. Two years ago my wife of seven years died, and I took her death very hard. When something like that happens, it makes you stop and take stock of your life. I felt I needed to get out of Toronto. I was raised in a farm village until I was twelve, and so I began looking around for a policeman's position in a small town. Your advertisement popped up conveniently in our station. And I applied."

"Very well put," Breezy breezed, as if he were an expert at adjudicating public speeches.

"You mentioned that you applied last year for a detective's job," Barwise said, glancing at the notes before him. "What was that all about?"

"Not much detecting to do in this place," Joiner muttered. "Not much of anything."

"Those are pretty high hopes," Breezy chipped in.

"Well, that was partly a reflection of my need for some sort of change in my life. I was quite happy being a patrolman, but as a youth I'd got two years of college in before I ran out of money, and so I felt I might be qualified for something more. I passed the detective exam, but then I saw your ad and I thought that it offered a more dramatic opportunity for change – and a return to my roots perhaps."

"That makes perfect sense to me," Maud said.

"So you'd like to be an ordinary village constable, then?" Barwise said.

"I think Mr. Garrett has made that clear," Breezy said, sensing the dialogue was escaping his grasp.

"Yes," Garrett said, "I think I would make a competent one. I have eight years of experience in policing at the street level. I get along with people well. I believe I could be of genuine service to you and your fellow villagers."

"Well, we're not exactly a metropolis," the Reeve said with obvious pride. "You won't find much crime to deal with hereabouts."

"What precisely would my responsibilities be?"

Again, there was an uncomfortable pause.

"Does anybody here know what Franny did with his time?" Breezy said with an embarrassed smile. "I know he stopped in to chat at the barber shop several times a day."

"And he was always at the fall fair," Joiner said.

"And all the other civic events," Breezy said, lest their guest think they had only a single, annual public gathering.

"Ball games and hockey matches," Joiner added. "He was a damn good umpire."

Miss Hannah blushed at the "damn" and her pencil stuttered.

"Actually, Franny Piersall was a man of regular habits," Barwise said. "He had a daily routine."

"That he did," Maud said, cutting Breezy off from his interjection. "Three times a day he went on a regular patrol that took him up and down every street, across to the freight-sheds and back down Edward Street where he checked on every business and shop. Then after supper he would check the locks on these same doors and make sure the town was safely asleep before he himself retired."

"He patrolled on his bicycle," Joiner said. "Rode like a maniac, if you ask me.."

"I don't recall asking you, Farley," the Reeve said.

"The bicycle would be part of your equipment," Barwise pointed out. "The village loaned it to Franny, some twenty years ago. It'll be parked beside the back door of the house."

"Indeed," the Reeve said loudly, "there is a rent-free house, a significant part of the stipend you will be offered. A fine, well-kept cottage on Elizabeth Ave. With Franny's furniture still in it."

"That all sounds fine," Garrett said, "but is there no crime at all in the village?"

"We've had a rash of bicycles stolen and ridden hard," Breezy said proudly. "And there's always kids playing hooky from school. That's a never-ending problem."

"And a drunk or two to be thawed out from time to time," Barwise said. "We use the cells below, but the keys were lost years ago, so you'd have to apply the honour system."

This time it was Joiner who flushed, and Garrett noticed now that his cheeks were red-veined and permanently scarlet – the legacy of some determined whiskey consumption.

"And we get a lot of riff raff off the boats," Breezy said with evident indignation. "Can't help it, being so close to the docks. Whenever a ship come in, Franny would appear like magic, and walk up and down Edward Street with his nightstick in full view."

"And, of course," Maud said, "we're used to treating Franny's house as the police station, where folks can come and make complaints about what's bothering them. And they expect their constable to be at home."

"It's a seven-day-a-week commitment, then?" Garrett said.

"Sundays are awful quiet," Joiner said. "Dead as doornail usually."

"More or less," Breezy said to Garrett. "But in between patrolling and any specific requests, your time is your own. Franny was a great reader, wasn't he, Miss Hannah?"

Miss Hannah blushed her answer.

"He even bought books," Joiner said, somewhere between awe and disapproval.

"And speaking of buying," Breezy said, "you're aware of the monthly salary? It's not much, but we're in the middle of a depression and times are hard. Many of my electoral supporters are on the dole."

"Fifty dollars, wasn't it?" Garrett said.

The Reeve flinched at the remark as if the money itself, in coinage, had struck him frontally.

"You wouldn't expect it all in hard cash, I presume," Breezy said with some alarm.

"I don't follow you," Garrett said.

"It's fifty dollars equivalent. If we haven't got the cash in a given month – depending on the amount of relief money we've got to dole out – we'll pay you in kind."

"Meaning foodstuffs, mostly," Maud said. "Including all the ice-cream sundaes you'd care to consume."

"I see your point. These are tough times."

"Is there anything more you'd like to ask us?" Barwise said.

"If not," Breezy said, "then we'd ask you to wait outside while my colleagues and I confer."

"I can't think of anything," Garrett said, "except to thank you for your attention and consideration of my application."

Maud Marsden walked him to the door.

"This shouldn't take long," she said with a smile.

Garrett sat down on the wooden steps. What on earth have I done? was the only thought racing through his head. I'm risking a well-paying job and probably a detective's career for a chance to do what? Keep watch on a sleepy and puffed-up little village that had little need for real policing. Still, he'd taken an instant liking to Max Barwise and Maud Marsden. There could be many others just like them waiting to make his acquaintance, holding out the possibility of changing his life for the better, and, if not obliterating the past, then at least assuaging its pain.

The door opened behind him.

"We've made up our minds," Maud said. "The job is yours if you want it. We've got a contract ready to be signed."

Garrett was taken aback. It had been less than five minutes. The most he had expected was that he would be told his candidacy was under serious consideration, that he had made the short list.

"What about the other candidates?" he sputtered.

Maud grinned knowingly. "There weren't any," she said.

Without thinking, Stan Garrett followed her inside.

# CHAPTER 2

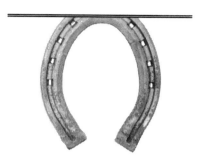

Stan Garrett moved into the deceased constable's house on Elizabeth Avenue on a Sunday evening in mid-September, nine days after the interview in the village library. In the interval he had said his goodbyes to his parents and his colleagues at the division. The latter threw him a going-away party that had about it more the air of a wake than a celebration. As far as his mates were concerned, Garrett might as well be moving to Timbuktu to do missionary work – Port Eddy seemed that exotic and forsaken in their big-city minds. He promised his parents that he would write to them faithfully every week.

As the house was fully furnished, he was able to travel very light, having stored some of the keepsakes from his marriage in his parents' garage. Thus it was with two suitcases in hand that he stepped away from the Petroleum City taxi and walked towards his new home. As he stepped inside, he thought he saw a curtain shift in the neighbour's window. His arrival had not gone unremarked.

The house itself had been cleaned and tidied in advance of his coming, and the closets and wardrobe had been emptied of Franny Piersall's lifelong possessions. Still, Garrett could feel the man's presence everywhere: there was no mistaking an inhabited abode whatever efforts had been made to exorcise its rightful resident. Garrett got more than a start when he entered the bedroom and nearly walked straight into a manikin dressed in a brand-new constable's uniform. (His measurements had been taken by a much-blushing Miss Hannah before he had left the interview.) On the dresser lay Franny Piersall's nightstick, his handcuffs and key, and a holster whose bulge suggested it held a revolver of some sort.

Garrett went over to these items, hefted the nightstick and found it to his liking (though he doubted it had ever been struck in anger) and inserted the key in the handcuffs' lock. He lifted the heavy holster, drew open a drawer, placed the weapon inside, and shut it up tightly.

He went through to the back kitchen intending to make himself a cup of tea when he heard the back door rattle. When he opened it, no-one was there. But sitting on the stoop was a large chocolate cake: the first installment on his "stipend."

The next morning Garrett decided to follow his predecessor's protocol and begin a series of patrols about this village he had chosen to kick-start his life. A well-travelled CCM bicycle sat next to the rear stoop. Its fenders were rusty and the chrome on its handle-bars chipped, but the chain had been well-oiled and kept ready for instant action. Garrett decided he would use it only for emergencies, should there ever be any. There were only seven or eight streets in the entire village, so a walkabout seemed the expedient way to get around and make sure his presence was known to friend and foe alike. He also intended to pause and talk to as many folks as he could along the way.

It was a glorious late-summer morning. A few of the leaves on the maple trees that lined every street were beginning to turn colour. He strolled east to Duke Street at the far end of the village, then north to Duchess Street, which ran parallel to the CNR rail line that marked the northern boundary of the village and kept Petroleum City from overrunning Port Eddy. He passed several mothers with small children and nodded politely to them. He didn't expect to meet very many men on a Monday morning, as any of those who were employed caught the seven-thirty bus that took them to the oil refinery or the rubber plant in the City. And those not employed would likely stay close to home, ashamed perhaps to show their faces too publicly. As he came to Princess Street, he spotted a leafy lane that must run behind the houses on that street. It reminded him of many such lanes in his childhood village where he and his pals would spend most of their free hours. He decided to go down the lane towards Edward Street, the main thoroughfare.

Just as he stepped onto the lane he noticed something even more intriguing. In a large maple behind the first house on Princess he was certain he spied a boy's tree-house. It was not readily visible, and anyone walking briskly along this part of the lane would not see it at all. But one corner of it jutted out behind a branch as it swung in the morning breeze. Garrett stood for a long while and let the bittersweet memories of his boyhood, all of which seemed to have happened two lives ago, wash over him.

"You must be Mr. Garrett, our new constable." The voice, high and melodious, came from a woman standing at her back gate only a few yards from Garrett. He turned and smiled.

"It must have been the uniform that gave me away," he said with a grin.

"We don't get too many like it hereabouts," she said, still smiling. "I hope you've been made welcome."

"There was a cake waiting," he said, coming over to her.

She was a woman not yet thirty with rich, reddish-brown hair and bright hazel eyes. She wore a kerchief loosely fitted over the abundance of her hair and a plain white apron over her flowered housedress.

"I'm Susan Shaw," she said. "I live here with my Uncle Wilbur and my young son."

Without a husband or a father for the son, he thought.

"I'm Stan Garrett. Pleased to meet you."

"I hope you'll get to like it here. Folks are friendly, but we've never known anyone but Franny to wear that uniform. It'll take some getting used to."

"I've got lots of time. I'm here for the long haul."

"Good. Well, then, I'll let you get on with your patrol."

Garrett might have preferred to linger longer, but Susan Shaw had just reminded him of his duty. He put his fingers to his cap and strode back to Duchess Street.

He walked west past Friar's Way down to Huron Street. He saw no-one except a sad-looking fellow on his front stoop with a battle of beer in one hand and a cigarette in the other. He did not wave. There were no houses on the west side of Huron, so Garrett could see right across the river flats to the point where lake and river met. A steam engine and its several box-cars were puffing along towards the freight-sheds beside the docks. He decided he would use the bicycle to patrol that area of the village later in the morning. Meantime he reached Edward Street, where he turned east again. Here before him were the many shops and businesses he was hired primarily to protect.

The Regency Arms, on the south-west corner of Huron and Edward, was shuttered tight. Garrett decided he would leave meeting its proprietor until his early-afternoon patrol when the taprooms would be open. From the look of the decaying, dust-covered upper windows, Garrett assumed there was little in the way of innkeeping carried on. Visitors from the ships would stay aboard overnight or move on to Petroleum City where there were proper hotels. But the Regency Arms would soon be busy with all those wishing to slake their thirst in it beverage rooms.

The first business entirely on Edward Street was Max Barwise's pool hall. The pool room itself would be open after lunch, but the outer shop, which sold cigarettes, pop and chocolate bars, was open for business and doing a brisk trade. Barwise spotted Garrett, and gave him a thumbs up.

Across the street a little farther up was Breezy Harker's barber shop, which Garrett decided to avoid for the present, but he did poke his head into the post office, where the postmistress was busy sorting mail behind a wicket. She looked up and gave Garrett a dazzling, predatory smile.

"My word, if it ain't the new constable! Do come all the way in and introduce yourself properly!" She dropped her packet of letters and stretched her hand across to seize Garrett's in a vice-like, overheated grip. "Ain't you a pretty sight for sore eyes!"

"Stan Garrett, ma'am."

"Good gracious, but I haven't been called 'ma'am' since somebody mistook me for a school marm. I'm Eunice Potter, the assistant postmistress of our little burg. I hear you've left the big city for Port Eddy."

"With few regrets, ma'am."

"Eunice, please."

"Eunice. I'm looking forward to being a part of this fine community."

"Well, you may not think it fine once you've gotten to know us," Eunice Potter chuckled.. She was a handsome woman in her mid-thirties with curly, bottle-blond hair, rouged cheeks and a scarlet, sensuous mouth. Her tiny blue eyes were piercing and appraising at the same time. Her voice was alto and forceful, as if it were always slightly louder in its reach than the room to which it was confined. She had several rings on several fingers, but none where a wedding band should be. It was hard to imagine that such a woman had been passed over for marriage unless she herself had wished it so or her opinion of her own worth had been unhappily overestimated.

"I'll be surprised if that happens," Garrett said. "But I'm just making my initial rounds and trying to put as many names to faces as I can."

"Well, then, I fully expect to see you on round number two."

Garrett smiled, nodded politely, and left.

As he was coming out of the post office, he spotted someone slipping into the alley between the post office and the grocer's next door. When he stepped over to take a look, he was surprised to see a thin stick of a man, shabbily dressed, slinking along the east wall of the post office. He kept his back to the wall at all times and continuously glanced left and right in a series of furtive gestures. Was the fellow preparing to break into one of the storerooms or sheds behind the businesses on this side of the street?

Whatever his intentions he soon disappeared behind the post office proper. Garrett moved quickly across in front of the grocery and peered down the alley on its eastern side. Sure enough, the fellow had crossed to this alley as well and had begun slinking, more slowly and furtively this time, with his back always to the wall, towards Edwards Street. Garrett jumped back so as not to be seen. Behind him he heard the front door of the store open, but he concentrated on the task at hand. Seconds later, he could hear the shuffle of the fellow's feet coming very close. Garrett stepped into the alley and seized the man by the collar.

A loud squealing protest erupted from the man's throat, but there were no words recognizable – only an eerie garble of which terror was the principal ingredient.

"Jesus! You've grabbed Sideways Slim!"

This warning came from Farley Joiner, the grocer-councillor, who had quickly come up to Garrett's side. Then he was bending over the wretched fellow, who had collapsed in a foetal heap and was babbling away to himself in a pathetic singsong rhythm.

"I'm sorry," Garrett said, abashed and baffled. "Who is he?"

"That's Sideways Slim Coote," Joiner said. "Shellshocked at the Somme. Got blasted by a grenade that landed too close to him."

"But I saw him skulking suspiciously behind your store."

"He can't move anywhere unless he's got his back to some wall or other – waiting for the next bomb, I suppose. He moves up and down the alleys that way, making his way along the street."

Joiner leaned down and said to Sideways Slim, "Going to the butcher shop, are ya, Slim?"

Slim nodded. His babbling stopped, but was replaced by a fierce trembling.

"This is the new constable, Mr. Garrett. He's here to protect us. He won't bother you again."

"I'm very sorry," Garrett said. To Joiner he said, "What'll we do with him now?"

"Just go away and let him be. He's almost where he's headed."

"Thanks for your help," Garrett said."

"Don't mention it. I just popped out for a smoke, but I'd better be getting back in. Mrs. Joiner's got me on the clock."

With that he went back inside and, reluctantly, Garrett left Sideways Slim to recover as best he could. Getting to know the inhabitants of Port Eddy was not going to be quite as simple as he had imagined.

Garrett crossed the street to say hello to Maurice Brandon, the eighty-year-old baker, who was sweeping off the sidewalk in front of his shop. He was as pale as the flour he worked with and so frail it appeared he might fall or be blown over should he release his grip on the broom. But if he could be friendly and cheerful after sixty years of baking, as he was, then Garrett felt there was hope for himself.

The library was closed, so he moved on to the intersection of Edward and King. It was ten o'clock, and he was glad to see that the dairy-bar was already open. He went in and found three men who looked as if they were sailors from some ship, sharing a banana-split with three spoons. Maud Marsden, looking much younger than her forty-five years, beamed him a smile.

"Right on schedule, I'd say," she laughed. "You'll be making old Franny happy, wherever he is now."

"I've managed to meet a number of townsfolk," Garrett said, taking a stool. "And they're making me feel quite welcome, which can't be all that easy for them."

"Or you, eh?"

"I'm doing okay. Right now I've worked up a thirst. I'll have a ginger-ale float."

"Coming right up."

She made the float quickly and expertly, and placed it before Garrett. "You'll get to meet the whole village, I suspect, this coming Saturday."

"Oh? How's that? Is it fall fair time already?"

"That's not for three weeks yet. No, what happens Saturday is more important than a dozen fairs."

"A circus coming to town?" He hadn't seen any posters in his walkabout.

"You might say that. It's the annual horseshoe contest between the village and the city – an event we've won for the past five years, I might add."

"What can be so earth-shattering about a horseshoe contest?"

Maud smiled broadly. "We love to beat Petroleum City, at anything, but particularly horseshoes. The winner of Saturday's contest goes on to the regional playdowns in London. We haven't made it past that hurdle, but we're quite content to humiliate the braggarts from the city that's been trying to annex us now for sixty years. They've got us surrounded, but we aren't about to surrender."

"Good for us, then." Garrett sipped on his float. "So I'll be doing crowd control, I expect." Garrett was quite familiar with the task as he had patrolled the Canadian National Exhibition on many occasions, and enjoyed it thoroughly.

"Oh, you'll be more than that," Maud said, suddenly serious. "I hope you know something about the game."

"As a matter of fact, I do. I was pretty good at it in my teens, but I must admit I haven't picked up a horseshoe in over ten years."

"Well, you won't be expected to play – we've got two wonders for that – but you will be asked to officiate some of the matches."

"Officiate? Oh my, that's quite a responsibility."

"It is. That's why each side uses a policeman to do the job. While they are hardly neutral, we've found them to be more than fair. There has never been a serious dispute in all the years we've been holding these matches, in part because our team has rarely let the opposition come close to a victory."

"I'm relieved to hear that. It would be strange if a policeman was the cause of a dispute instead of the arbiter."

"I'm sure Breezy Harker will be around to your house tonight to read you chapter and verse about Saturday. But you might as well make sure you go behind the Regency Arms on your patrol after supper. The team and their supporters will be practising there."

"Yes. I'd prefer to volunteer."

"I can't think of a better way for the town to get a gander at you and see what a fine fellow we've taken on as constable."

Garrett barely kept himself from blushing. "Thank you for that," he said, "and for the float. It was superb."

On his afternoon patrol Garrett met the rest of the businessmen along Edward Street and several more residents who stopped to say hello and introduce themselves. He went into the library – open two afternoons and three evenings a week – and thanked Miss Hannah for taking his measurements and relaying them to the tailor. Even with walking every street in the village, the patrol took just under an hour to complete. That left him with much time on his hands. Fortunately Franny Piersall had been a voracious reader and purchaser of books. In the little den, where his predecessor's incident-book was kept, Garrett found a cache of mystery novels. He recognized many of the names: Christie,

Hammet, Allingham, Sayers. He would have no difficulty whiling away the hours that remained crime-free.

He was planning to do some grocery shopping but discovered that someone had filled his cupboard with many of the staples he needed, and just as he was thinking a trip to the butcher's might be useful, he heard a familiar noise at the back door. There on his stoop sat a cloth-covered dish. He looked left and right, but his benefactor had vanished. Under the cloth, still warm, was a shepherd's pie – enough for several meals.

While he enjoyed the shepherd's pie immensely and the homemade peanut butter cookies he found in the cupboard, he did not enjoy eating alone. After Anna died, he had tried living by himself for several months, but found the loneliness unbearable. So, against his better judgement he had moved back in with his parents. They were kind and solicitous of his well-being, but he soon realized he needed solitude to grieve fully and try to imagine a future without his beloved. But he didn't have the heart then to tell his parents or suggest that he merely move out. In some way that he didn't really understand, his need to get away and be alone was both overwhelming and absolutely necessary.

After supper he decided to carry out two patrols. The first, on the old CCM, would be a broad sweep of the perimeter of the town, including a careful survey of the docks and any ships that might have arrived during the day. Earlier he had met the shed foreman and several of the stevedores who lived in the village, but he had found the long walk to the docks a waste of time, as there was nothing between them and the town proper but fields on one side and a vast swamp on the other. The bicycle would do nicely for this part of the patrol, as well as provide a quick trip through the Queen's Bush that hugged and gave shape to the north-east sector of the village. His second patrol, later, would be his regular route on foot.

The cycling excursion went unperturbed by anything other than a bright or desultory "hello" here and there. On the subsequent walkabout he deliberately went down the alley beside the Regency Arms and around to the back, drawn there by the clink of horseshoes hitting their mark. Garrett rounded a corner, and took in the scene before him.

It was idyllic. The sun was low in the west and cast elongated, shimmering shadow across an impeccably laid out set of horseshoe pits, a neat square with a steel post in the exact centre at either end. Two men were standing at the far end, horseshoes in their right hand, bathed in sunlight. A crowd of close to a dozen people, as if stilled by prayer, stood motionless along the route the horseshoe would take. As Garrett approached, one of the two men held the horseshoe up to his face as if sighting some distant prey, then rocked and stepped forward. The horseshoe left his hand as softly as a feather and seemed to float on invisible wings towards the distant pit, turning around and around in tight, purposeful circles until it clanged against the post, metal on metal, spun like a dervish and settled around it as delicately as a necklace. A cheer went up from the worshipping throng.

Then silence again as the second player stepped forward and pitched his missile skyward. It too whirled, and seemed to hesitate before it struck, spun and settled. Another cheer.

"Good shootin', Harold!"

"Nice shot, Clem!"

Garrett's presence was soon noted and Breezy Harker came forward and greeted him. "It's Constable Garrett, folks. He'll be officiating at the match on Saturday."

Then he whispered to Garrett, "You do know how horse-shoes is played, don't you?"

"I do, and I'd be honoured to referee on Saturday."

"Have you met our champion duo yet?" Breezy said, drawing Garrett into the throng.

"I waved at them this afternoon, yes," Garrett said, shaking hands with Harold Cooper, proprietor of the confectionary store and gas-pump, and Clem Murphy, the postmaster and fire chief.

"Ain't been beaten in five years," someone shouted.

Breezy attempted to introduce Garrett to the members of the crowd, but their names slipped in and out of his mind. It would take time, he thought, but it was not impossible that within a month he would be able to name every one of the town's six hundred and fifty souls. Just as Clem and Harold were about to resume their friendly match, a new arrival made his way into the throng.

"Sorry I'm late. What's the score?" he said.

"Just getting started, Wilbur," Breezy said. "Have you met our new constable, Stan Garrett?"

"I'm Wilbur Bright," the newcomer said. He was a robust-looking older man, well past retirement age, with a shock of white hair that was as smooth and neat as a helmet. His eyes were an intense blue, as if the world always bore watching.

"You must be Susan's uncle, then?" Garrett said, remembering that Susan Shaw had mentioned she lived with her uncle and her son.

"My, but you're a right detective, young fellow," Uncle Wilbur said with an approving grin. "You've found me out already."

"Glad to meet you, sir."

They shook hands.

Breezy then said to Wilbur loud enough for the denizens of the beverage rooms to hear, "You've come to bring us news, then?"

Uncle Wilbur frowned. "I have."

"Good news like the gospel, I take it?"

"I'm not so sure."

At this, Clem, Harold and all the others drew closer and strained to catch every word.

"What do you mean by that?"

"Well, the City are putting up Tug Mason."

"No surprise there."

"But the second player is."

"Who?" Clem Murphy asked. "Not Bolt or Lester?"

"Somebody new – a fella named Ray Stanton."

"The name sounds familiar," Breezy said.

"It ought to," Uncle Wilbur said. "He was a champion tosser twenty years ago, when he was barely seventeen."

"That's right," Harold Cooper said. "My dad saw him play when I was just a kid. Told me he was dynamite."

"But he went squirrely in the head, didn't he?" Breezy said hopefully. "Won the City championship once, but wasn't seen again."

"Something like that," Cooper said. "So they're bringing him out of retirement to play with Tug Mason, eh? Sounds to me like they're desperate."

"Or conniving," Breezy said, who, being a conniver himself, was quick to recognize the breed. "You don't suppose they're trying to bring in a ringer and pass him off as one of their own?"

"The player must be resident in the community for three years prior to the match," Murphy explained to Garrett.

"And as our official, Mr. Garrett, you'll have to check the legitimacy of any claims they make," Breezy said.

"They'll need a birth certificate and proof of address, I presume," Garrett said, taken aback by this turn of events but certainly not wishing to show it.

"I can help you out there," Uncle Wilbur said. "I'm older than any of you, and I was present at the City championship when young Ray Stanton won the prize. I'll remember him well. And if it is him, we can be sure he's at least City born and bred. But if it should turn out to be a ringer, I'll soon know."

A ringer, Garrett knew, was a hot-shot brought in from outside the community to bolster the local team – in this case illegally.

"I wouldn't put anything past them devils from the City," Breezy said. "But with you and Mr. Garrett here watching out for us, and Clem and Harold pitching perfect, as they always do, we can't lose, can we?"

Garrett shuddered. In his view, statements like that invariably came back to haunt you.

As Garrett walked back to Edward Street, Max Barwise came out of his pool hall to say hello. Garrett was sure the man had been waiting for him.

"So you've seen our champion tossers, I take it?" he said.

Garrett smiled and tried not to look at the armless sleeve. "That I have."

"And Breezy has commandeered you to officiate on our behalf?"

"Right after he said 'hello.'"

"I hope it's not too much of an imposition," Barwise said, then added, "I stopped you because I wanted to tell you how important this tournament is to the village."

"I'm getting a sense of just how much already."

"It'll be held in front of the grandstand at the racetrack and fair grounds. There'll be several hundred people there, including most of our population. There'll be a pipe band from Forest and concession stands. The mayor will be there beside our reeve pretending to believe in fair play and proclaiming the best team ought to win, et cetera."

"I see."

"And winning is important to the village as well. We've got three dozen families on relief and several dozen more who are underemployed. They've taken two or three pay cuts since 1929. If Farley Joiner didn't extend credit, there'd be children starving in this town. Fortunately the trade we get from the boats keeps our businesses afloat, so we are in a position to help as much as we can."

"But we cannot live by bread alone, scarce as it may be?"

"Exactly. We need our diversions and small delights. We need to feel that something is going right for a change, that David sometimes defeats Goliath."

"And do we have a champion team?"

"Clem Murphy and Harold Cooper are the best. They've won these matches and done well in the regionals in London for five years running."

"Breezy and Wilbur Bright seemed to fear that Petroleum City might try to bring in a ringer and pass him off as a local."

"They're desperate enough, but it's not an easy thing to do. Besides, we've got you to rely on, haven't we?"

Garrett smiled. "That's what I'm afraid of."

As Garrett entered his house, he could hear the phone ringing: one long and two short – his number. He dashed to the kitchen and picked the receiver off its hook.

"Police house. Constable Garrett speaking."

For a moment there was no sound at the other end of the line. Then the stunted, laboured breathing of someone trying to find their voice.

"B-burglar! I've got a burglar at my door!"

# CHAPTER 3

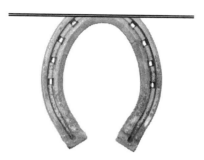

The frantic caller managed somehow to give Garrett her name – Prudence Shannon – and her address – 47 Princess Street – before returning to her stuttered and garbled "B-burglar." That address would make her house very close to Susan Shaw's, if he remembered correctly.

"Don't worry, ma'am. I'll be there in two minutes," he said.

He dashed to his back stoop and hopped on the elderly CCM. It responded heroically. He peddled down Elizabeth to Princess Street and wheeled north. Moments later he pulled up on the lawn of number 47. It was two doors down from Susan Shaw's place. There was no light shining on the front porch, so he trotted to the back door and rapped gently, making sure he looked all about in case the burglar was lurking nearby. But he saw or heard nothing in the shadowy dark. He rapped again, more loudly. At last there came from behind the door a wee squeak of a voice.

"Yes, who's there?"

"It's me, Miss Shannon. Constable Garrett. Please open up."

Very slowly and, it seemed, reluctantly, the door eased open.

"Miss Shannon?"

"Prudence. Oh, I am glad to see you, sir."

The door opened wide to reveal a small, spare lady with paper-thin skin and wispy grey hair imprisoned in steel curlers.

"I'm Constable Garrett. And Stan will do fine."

"Oh, I've had such a fright, Constable."

"I'm not surprised if you caught a burglar in the act."

"Please, come in. I'll make us a cup of tea and tell you what I saw."

"Thank you, no, ma'am."

"You won't come in?"

"I won't have any tea."

"But I've got the kettle on the boil," she said without a trace of disingenuousness.

Despite her fright, Garrett thought, she had had the wherewithal to prepare tea.

"In that case . . ."

He followed her down a shadowy hall to her kitchen, where, set out upon the table were a pair of cups and saucers and a teapot with the lid off awaiting the boiling water from the stove – as if she were about to entertain the vicar at high tea.

"Did the fellow actually get inside?" Garrett said, sitting down.

"Oh, no. Nothing so horrible as that," Prudence said as she poured boiling water over the leaves. "Do you take cream?"

"Clear is fine." Garrett waited until he had taken a sip of tea and nodded approval at his hostess, then he said, "Where did you see this fellow, then?"

"In my sewing-room," she said, and her teacup began to shake at the sudden reminder of her terrifying experience. Her eyes were round and luminous, as if they had refused to shrivel with the rest of her frail body.

"Then he did get in?" Garrett said, puzzled.

"I mean, Constable, that I was in my sewing-room. I live here alone and I sit in there and listen to the nine o'clock news every evening. That's when I heard a tap at the window."

"A tap? That's odd. Burglars are usually as quiet as cats."

"It was a double rap, not loud – I wouldn't have heard it if I hadn't been sitting ten feet away. It gave me such a start."

"Did you see the fellow?"

"I looked over – naturally." She took a slow sip of her tea to calm herself.

"And saw?"

"A man's face peering in at me – bold as brass."

"Just peering?"

"Yes. Just peering. Then I screamed and the face disappeared."

"You did the right thing. Burglars are actually sneak thieves. They usually shy away at the first sign they might be discovered. I'm sure he's well away from here by now."

"Oh, I do hope so. But I feel much safer now that you're here."

"Do you think he was testing the window to see if it could be opened?"

"Oh, dear me. I never thought of that. I must see that all my windows are locked."

"Yes. And I advise you to keep a light on over both your back and front porches. Burglars prefer the dark."

"I don't like to use the electricity – my brother Melvin left me this house when he died, but not much else. But if you think I should do so, then of course I'll do it. And I must say that you came here twice as quick as dear old Franny, God rest his soul."

"You've had burglars before?" Garrett put down his tea.

"Oh, yes. They seem to have a particular liking for this house. But Franny Piersall was never able to catch any of them. What do you make of that?"

"Do you have anything of value here? Family heirlooms? Old stamps?"

"Only my Royal Doulton figurines. That's what puzzles me, Constable. Why do burglars insist on picking this house?"

"Perhaps I'd better have a look outside," Garrett said.

"Oh, but you must have a second cup of tea, and an oatmeal cookie."

After a second cup of tea and two cookies – during which time Prudence Shannon explained what an important person her brother Melvin had been at the refinery in Petroleum City, working in the office and flourishing a clean, freshly starched white shirt every day – Garrett was able to slip outside and, using his flashlight, carefully examine the ground at the rear of the house for footprints. But it was very dry and there was little evidence, one way or another, that anyone had stood near the sitting-room window. However, a branch of the hedge at the near corner leading to the house that sat between the Shannon place and Susan Shaw's, had a broken twig. The break was fresh. It could have been made by the burglar escaping through the hedge or by some child or dog wandering about earlier in the day. Perhaps there were children next door.

He went back in. "There's no sign of him, ma'am. No footprints. But burglars, as I said, are like cats – they rarely leave any trace of their travels."

"Are you sure you won't stay for a bit? I do feel safe with you here."

"I should go next door to see if the folks over there saw anything."

"There'll only be Wilma Turnidge, on her own, like me. Her husband works the afternoon shift, four to twelve, at the refinery."

"I'll knock gently, then."

Prudence Shannon smiled – her luminous, sad, frightened eyes lit by something brighter, safer. "I'll leave the porch light on," she said.

Garrett slipped through a break in the hedge and went up to the rear door of the Turnidge house He knocked discreetly, noticing as he did that there seemed to be only one faint light showing on the second floor above him, a bathroom night light perhaps. He waited for thirty seconds and knocked again. He heard an inner door open, then a chain being pulled off its latch. For a sleepy village with little crime, the citizens certainly were zealous about locking themselves in at night. Perhaps there was more going on here than he had been led to believe.

The rear door opened several inches. "Oh, it's you, Constable."

"Mrs. Turnidge?"

"That's right. As you can see, I was just going to bed. Is there something I can help you with?"

Wilma Turnidge was dressed in a flowered kimono, and her rich, chestnut curls flowed freely about her face, unbound by curler or clasp. She looked to be about thirty-five years of age, but it was her obvious femininity that attracted and held one's attention. Her eyes were dark and bold and sensuous. At the moment she was flushed, having run down the stairs perhaps.

"My apologies, ma'am, but Miss Shannon has reported seeing a burglar lurking about her place and there's a possibility he escaped through this property. I was wondering if you had seen or heard anything?"

Wilma Turnidge laughed out loud. "Oh, Constable, that poor soul sees burglars everywhere! Franny Piersall refused to come in the end. I'm sorry you've been called out here for nothing."

"I see. You think this was a figment of Miss Shannon's imagination?"

"I do, and so does anyone who knows her. But then you can't be expected to know the oddities of folks around here, can you?"

"So you saw or heard nothing?"

"Nothing."

They had been talking through a six-inch crack in the doorway, so that the space seemed to be filled with Wilma's attractive face and sweetly curved kimono. He wasn't about to be invited in for tea at this house.

"Well, thank you, ma'am. Sorry to have disturbed you."

"Good night, Constable." The door closed with a finite click. A bolt was shoved into place. Garrett stood on the stoop for a moment, and saw the upstairs light go out.

He looked over to Susan Shaw's house. It was ablaze with light. Suddenly a figure appeared on the back porch.

"Is that you, Constable Garrett?" Susan Shaw called out.

"Yes, I'm just off back home."

"Well, come in and have a cup of tea, won't you?"

Garrett hesitated but, feeling he had done more than his duty this evening, he walked across the lawn adjoining the two properties and said, "I'd love a cup of tea."

They were in the comfortable living-room of Susan's home – Susan, Garrett and Uncle Wilbur. Davie, Susan's ten-year-old son, was asleep upstairs.

"Yes," Uncle Wilbur was saying, "I spent thirty-five years on the Great Lakes, the last five as captain of the Fort William, the biggest of the Imperial Oil tankers."

"It must have been an exciting life," Garrett said, not without envy.

"Routine and boring most of the time, son, but I've been through a few storms in my day. Then things get exciting – and scary."

"Were you involved in the great storm of 1913?"

"Yes, he was," Susan said, trying, not for the first time, to enter the conversation. "And his ship went down."

"I was one of the lucky ones. We were rescued before it sank."

Even though Uncle Wilbur was dominating the conversation, Garrett and Susan took every opportunity to glance slyly at one another, liking what they saw. Susan's dark red hair and hazel eyes were enough to attract any man, but it was the overall effect of intelligence and wholesomeness that really riveted Garrett's attention: she was the archetypal girl next door. Garrett, of course, rarely examined himself in a mirror, but he was six feet tall, brown-haired and handsome in a rugged way – especially in his uniform.

Some details of the rescue and the fury of the infamous storm followed, then Susan said nicely, "Uncle, would you mind checking on Davie? He's not been sleeping well lately."

Uncle Wilbur gave Susan an odd look, but got up happily enough and headed for the stairs.

"He's a dear," Susan said, "but he's also an old sea-salt and likes to spin a yarn, especially with an audience outside of the old fogies who people Breezy Harker's barber shop."

"I enjoyed his talk very much."

"You're too polite to say otherwise, but it's true that I am worried about Davie."

"In what way?"

"Well, ever since his father died, almost a year ago, he hasn't been himself. He was a happy, good-natured child with a generous heart. But lately he's started to act out."

"I'm sorry to hear about your husband."

"Mike left for the West two years ago to try and find work. He had some luck on a farm in Saskatchewan and sent us back enough money to get by on. Uncle Wilbur has a decent pension and helps out, bless him."

"These are terrible times."

"But Mike was killed in some sort of accident or other. The boy felt he'd been abandoned when Mike left, despite me telling him over and over that his father was working for both of us, and would come back as soon as he could."

"He wrote the boy?"

"He did, but he wasn't a great letter writer, I'm afraid. Davie has the few letters tucked away in his dresser, but since Mike died, he hasn't taken them out. He seems to have seen his dad's death as more of a betrayal than his leaving us."

Garrett looked across at her. "He's only a lad. That's the way kids see the world, I suspect. But he'll grow out of it. Give it time."

"I hope so. Just this morning, before school, Uncle Wilbur tried to help Davie fix his broken bicycle. Uncle isn't too good with his hands and made a bit of a mess of things. Davie blew up at him and called him a useless old coot. He later apologized, under duress, though I think he was genuinely sorry."

"I wouldn't punish him too severely, though. Sounds to me as if he's hurting enough already."

"You have no children?"

"No, though Anna and I did try."

"Anna?"

"She passed away two years ago. That's one of the reasons I packed up and left Toronto."

"Too many memories?"

"Something like that."

Garrett was surprised at how much at ease he was, sitting here and talking with Susan Shaw, especially about Anna.

"I guess we're more or less in the same boat," Susan said. "But then I do have Davie."

"And Davie isn't in his bed!" Uncle Wilbur cried, dashing into the room, his neat white hair suddenly askew.

"Oh, no," Susan said. "I hope he hasn't run away again."

"Maybe he's just in the fort," Uncle Wilbur said hopefully.

"The tree-house out behind?" Garrett said.

"Yes," Susan said. "It's his refuge, where he goes when he's feeling the world hates him."

"I'll go have a look," Garrett said.

"Would you?"

Garrett went to the back door and stepped into the yard. The moon was almost full, so there was plenty of light washing down the lane behind the house. Garrett crossed the lane and looked up in the large maple directly opposite. A set of steps had been nailed to the far side of the trunk, leading up to a platform above. Garrett started up.

"Davie, are you there? It's Mr. Garrett. Your mom's worried that you're not in bed on a school night."

No answer.

Something made Garrett continue climbing. He poked his head through the entry-hole in the platform. Davie Shaw was fast asleep on an old blanket. Garrett came all the way up, gathered the boy in his arms and, with some difficulty, managed to ferry him to the ground without waking him.

Susan and Uncle Wilbur were waiting on the back porch.

"I found him sound asleep," Garrett whispered.

"Thank God for that. And thank you," Susan said.

"I'll carry him back to bed," Uncle Wilbur said, much relieved.

"And I'll say good night," Garrett said. "Thanks for the tea."

"Good night, then, Constable."

"Stan, please."

"Good night, Stan," Susan said, and it was music to the constable's ears.

Riding home, it occurred to Garrett that he'd had time today to read but two chapters of his Agatha Christie. It looked as if boredom would not be the principal component of his new job.

The Tuesday morning patrol went without incident, for which Garrett was grateful. He did stop briefly at Prudence Shannon's house to check again for footprints in the bright sunlight. He found none. While it was probably true that Prudence tended to fantasize burglaries, her fear on the phone had been genuine. Garrett was not fully convinced that no-one had peered into her sewing-room window. More likely they were dealing with a peeping Tom rather than a burglar. The Shannon house was an inappropriate target for any self-respecting second-storey man.

When, a little while later, he walked past the Regency Arms, the proprietor hailed him from the doorway to the Ladies and Escorts. This was Hopalong Hitchins, whom he had met the day before on his evening patrol. Hopalong was a squat little man with a beer belly and a gimpy left leg. His eyes looked as if they had been forcefully shut and had to fight continually to remain even marginally open.

"I wanted to give you a heads-up for this afternoon," Hopalong said in what passed for a conspiratorial whisper.

What now? Garrett thought.

"The Upper Lakes, an iron-carrier, is dockin' here for a day. Comin' in this afternoon, she is."

"Is that bad news?"

"It's crewed by a gang of toughs, who'll be in here drinkin' this afternoon and, after the supper break, all evenin' to boot. I'd be grateful if you stepped into the Men's Room this afternoon and again after supper. Let 'em get a gander at your nightstick, if ya take my meanin'."

"Show the colours, as it were," Garrett said.

"They need to know you're nearby and fully armed."

"You're expecting them to get into a brawl?"

"Mostly it's just foul language an' braggin', but I'd like to keep it that way. The sight of you ought to put the frightener on them, a lot more than poor old Franny could do in his last years. I told Breezy he had to hire a six-footer with a mean eye."

"I'll try to look mean," Garrett said, tipped his cap, and left the innkeeper to his riotous thoughts.

As arranged, Garrett did stop at the Regency Arms about two o'clock that afternoon. The Men's Room was jammed – with divers strangers off the boats, the crew of the Upper

Lakes (a noisy clutch in one corner), and a smattering of the unemployed who had a dime or two for a draft that could be nursed for an hour of forgetfulness. But it was not the sailors who were giving Hopalong and his waiter trouble. It was two men seated across from one another at a table near the bar. Their loud exchange was audible above the steady buzz in the room.

"You heard me, you bastard. I said you're to keep your filthy hands off of Wilma."

"You're crazy. You think every man in town has got the hots for your precious wife."

"Not everybody. Just you."

"I spoke to Wilma on the street. She said hello. What was I to do, snub her?"

"You accusin' her of bein' fresh with guys?" Wilma's defender, who had to be Orville Turnidge, was flushed scarlet with rage. He was a muscled fellow of middle eight with an extra large head and a sheaf of tight, black curls. His dark eyes blazed, and he raised a fist to pound it on the table.

"She's a fine, friendly woman, that's all. And if you didn't keep her walled up like some bird in that cage of a house, you and her'd be a sight better off."

"Don't tell me what to do, you son of a bitch!" Turnidge raised both fists now. "You want to settle this right here and now?"

"No-one's going to settle anything," Garrett said, striding up to the table, with a grateful proprietor suddenly limping in his wake. "Not here nor anywhere else."

"Who the fuck are you?" Turnidge cried, then realized, too late, that it was not a Salvation Army officer he was staring at but a police constable.

Garrett reached out and grabbed Turnidge by one wrist. "Just calm down, Mr. Turnidge and everything will be all right. I suggest you get up quietly and leave these premises."

"Let 'em fight it out!" one of the sailors shouted.

Garrett stared hard at Turnidge. Most of the rage had gone out of him. He looked a bit forlorn, but not beaten. "Okay, officer. I don't much feel like sitting opposite Mr. Dalton here. He gives off an odour."

"Out – now!" Garrett said.

"All right, I'm going."

Turnidge walked slowly to the door. There he turned and gave a thumbs-up to the crew of the Upper Lakes. They cheered.

"Welcome to Port Eddy," Hopalong said with a grim smile. "Nice town we've got here, eh?"

Garrett said to the object of Turnidge's abuse, "You'll be all right, Mr. Dalton?"

"Yes. And it's Fred Dalton. Thanks for keeping that maniac off me. I never saw a man so jealous of his wife."

"Wilma Turnidge?"

"Yes. And there never was a woman who deserved it less."

"I can vouch for that," Hopalong said. "The woman is left alone every afternoon and evening of the week, and not a complaint or an improper move out of her."

"Well, I'll keep a close watch on the Turnidge place," Garrett said.

And, if things continued in the fashion of his first two days on the job, a close watch on Prudence Shannon and Davie Shaw as well. Susan he could watch without cause.

# CHAPTER 4

On the Friday evening of the week before Stan Garrett began his duties as constable, an event of some importance had taken place in Petroleum City. Several hundred citizens had gathered in the bleachers of Tecumseh Park to watch a horseshoe match that would determine the second member of the team that was to play Port Eddy on the Saturday of the next week. The first member had already been selected: Tug Mason, who had won the City championship in August. But a number of tossers had shown well in that event, and so a series of elimination or showdown matches was scheduled to choose the second member. Only two players were now left in that series, Archie Bolt and Matt Lester. They were playing a two-out-of three set this Friday evening.

Besides the prestige of winning the county against Point Edward and the trophy symbolic of that win, Mayor

Portland Gage had added a monetary inducement to the mix. Although these contests were strictly amateur, the local refinery had secretly offered the mayor two hundred dollars to be given to the players after the event – as an "honorarium" – should the Petroleum City team win. If not, the pretence of amateurism would be religiously observed. These monies would be disbursed well under the table, as such inducements risked forfeiture of the matches. However, it was assumed that one hundred dollars per player, in the midst of a great depression, would provide plenty of incentive to silence on the matter. Thus, as Bolt and Lester battled to a one-all tie after two games, to the feverish excitement of the crowd, there was a lot more on the line than pride and prestige.

While the two contestants sat on a bench and rested up for the start of match three, a stranger came onto the grounds, sauntered up to one of the pits, picked up two horseshoes, and began tossing them at the far post. They had a peculiar hum to their arcing through the air and a decisive, almost impudent, ring as they struck the post and encircled it. Two more shoes followed the first pair. Then the fellow sauntered to the far pit, picked up several shoes and repeated the performance. Not a single shoe missed its mark. It was as if they were on strings and the tosser their puppeteer. One did threaten to become a leaner, but as if at some silent command, it tipped back slowly and settled down as a ringer.

By this time the crowd had stopped buzzing and milling. It was now fixated on the bold fellow whose horseshoes hummed with authority. Even Bolt and Lester were watching in awe as shoe after shoe found its mark.

The tosser himself was really quite nondescript. A man in his mid-thirties perhaps, he was of medium build with plain brown hair and grey eyes. His dress was casual, with threadbare patches on his pants and the elbows of his shirt. His expression was almost bored or indifferent, which gave what was happening to his horseshoes even more an air of the miraculous. This fellow, it seemed, with minimum concentration could throw nothing but ringers.

The spell was broken when Mayor Gage, manager of the City's team, stepped quietly up to the fellow and said, "That's quite a pitch you've got there, son. Where'd you learn it?"

"Right here in Petroleum City," the fellow replied, seemingly uninterested.

The Mayor's eyes lit up. "You mean to say you're a citizen of our town?"

"Lived here all my life."

"And you've not participated in any of our championship matches?" the Mayor said with disbelief.

By this time, Tug Mason, Archie Bolt and Matt Lester had come up and were staring hard at the interloper, not without a touch of annoyance, and envy.

"Not for a long time," the stranger said.

"Where you been, then?" Bolt said. He was a big, strong, outgoing sort. "Holdin' your light under a bushel basket?"

"Can you throw like that in a real game?" said Lester, a thin, nervous man with bulging eyes.

"I throw like that all the time," the interloper said evenly, as if he were stating the obvious.

"Well, it's too late to come bargin' in here and showin' off," Bolt said with more hope than conviction.

"You said 'not for a long time'," the Mayor said, cutting Bolt off. "I don't recall you ever participating in our playdowns."

"That's because it was almost twenty years ago. When I was seventeen."

"My God," Lester cried, "you can't be – "

"I am. I'm Ray Stanton."

The name was repeated by Lester, the Mayor and those nearest the stranger, and worked its way up to the bleachers, where it was repeated like a wind rustling through leaves.

"But you're dead!" the Mayor felt constrained to point out.

"I've been ill for many years. I live alone on Maxville Street in the house my parents left me. I practice tossing in my back yard – when I have the energy."

"It is you, ain't it?" Bolt said. "I was at the match when you won the City trophy. You was just a kid, a boy wonder. I never forget a face."

"W-why have you come here tonight?" Lester said, his voice nearly failing him.

"Just to watch. I thought nobody'd mind if I threw between matches. I'll rake the pits, if you like."

"You'll do nothing of the sort," the Mayor said. "Anyone who can throw ringers like that deserves a chance to vie for the spot still open on our squad."

"But what about our rules?" Bolt said, his face reddening.

"I make our rules," the Mayor said. He turned to Ray Stanton. "Would you be willing to play off with these fellows?"

"I don't want to interfere – "

"I decide what's interference," the Mayor said. "We want to beat Port Eddy on Saturday, don't we fellows? We've got to put out our two best tossers. Would you, Ray my boy, give it a try?"

"Very well," Stanton said matter of factly, as if he were agreeing to eat his spinach at supper. "If you like."

"But Matt and me are set to toss our final game!" Bolt protested.

"This ain't fair," Lester added.

"You're not saying you're afraid to play against Ray here, are you?"

What could Bolt and Lester say: they were afraid of no-one.

The Mayor turned to the crowd. "Would you folks like to see a former City champion participate in these playdowns?"

The roar of approval was vastly satisfying to a man accustomed to getting his own way.

"I'll play them both at the same time," Stanton suggested without a trace of boastfulness. "If I lose to either, I'll drop out, and if both beat me, the one with the highest score will be the overall winner. That way we can complete the match before dark."

"Any way you want it," the Mayor said.

"And we'll see how good you are when the pressure's on," Bolt said.

Even if Stanton lost, the Mayor was thinking, it would put the other two on their mettle. He wanted to win the contest against Port Eddy more than he wanted re-election. It had been five embarrassing years that saw the upstart village get too big for its britches and lord it over their betters.

With the crowd abuzz now, Bolt went to one pit and Lester the other. Stanton was to walk back and forth, playing an end with each in turn. The scoreboard, the one used for softball games, recorded the dual scores as they progressed.

Stanton played with the same nonchalance he had exhibited during his practice performance. Every time Bolt or Lester put on a ringer, Stanton covered it. Finally, the pressure would get to his opponent, and when it became clear that this onetime wunderkind was hardly ever going to miss, nerves frayed and deliveries wobbled. It was all over in an embarrassingly short time. Neither Lester nor Bolt scored a point. The second member of the City's squad had been chosen – virtually self-selected. The crowd cheered him to the echo and back. A Samson had been found to lead them against their enemies.

"My God," the Mayor breathed to the blond consort he had brought with him. "We've got ourselves a legitimate ringer." This circumstance seemed beyond the miraculous.

He went up and shook Stanton's hand. The fellow's demeanour had not changed. "You've made our squad, sir, and Lord help the Port Eddyans."

"You'll want to see my birth registration," Stanton said, pulling out a creased sheet of paper.

"A formality only. Yes, yes, this seems to be in order. And we have Mr. Bolt's recollection of your winning at age seventeen."

"And my residence had been in the City directory for many years."

"Good, good." The Mayor was beside himself with joy and anticipation.

But two members of the throng now surrounding the legitimate ringer were not particularly pleased.

"This is unfair," Lester complained to Bolt.

"That bastard just walks in here and plays one lucky match, and is gonna waltz off with our hundred dollars." Bolt and Lester, whoever won tonight, had agreed to split the money, should one of them help to win the trophy next week. Their carefully laid plan was now in ruins.

"Maybe he'll fall on his face next Saturday."

"Right now," Bolt snarled, "I'd like to rearrange it."

When Garrett got back from his Wednesday morning patrol, his phone was ringing.

"Police house. Garrett speaking."

"Stan, it's Susan."

"What's the matter?" He could hear the anxiety in her voice.

"The principal just called from the school, checking to see if Stevie was sick."

"And he isn't?"

"No. I sent him off to school at eight-thirty. He never arrived."

"I'm sure he's just playing hooky," Garrett said soothingly.

"But I've checked the fort and he's not there."

"It's a fine, warm day. He's probably headed off to Queen's bush or the river flats."

"You make it sound as if we're in Tom Sawyer's world," Susan said with an edge to her voice. "This is serious. He should be in school. This is his third time. And that means the strap." Her voice quavered.

"Oh, my. Well, I'd better find him first, hadn't I?"

There was a pause at the other end. "Would – would you consider bringing him here rather than the school? I'd – I'd like to deal with him myself first."

"I can do that. After all, you are his parent."

"Thank you."

"Any place besides the fort where he's likely to go?"

"Not near the river, I hope. He doesn't swim well."

"Don't worry. I'm on the case."

Garrett rang off. He hopped on his bicycle and did a slow circuit of the village, calling Davie's name softly as he went. He got no response. He pedalled slowly through Queen's bush, looking left and right as he wound his way along the path through it. He got off at the river flats and walked along the shoreline, impressed by the blue surge of the Great Lake into the narrows of the river. Across the river lay the United States, a half-mile and a country away. There was no sign of the boy.

Garrett tried to imagine what it would be like to be ten years old and fatherless. He had been blessed with two good parents, still very much alive and part of his life. Stevie was likely in some private space, he figured – if not his hideaway fort, then something very like it. He went back into the village proper, scoured every lane and alley, then went to the southern edge of town and spent fifteen minutes in Bayside Park. There were lots of potential "nests" here, but no Stevie. He stared across at the marsh, its cattails clicking in the warm breeze. No boy would enter it except during some spirited play with his pals.

Feeling defeated, inadequate, and not a little fearful, Garrett rode back to Susan's, intending to relay the bad news. Perhaps the boy had returned to school to face the music. He hoped so.

Deciding to approach by the back door, he entered the lane and parked by the low rear fence. He thought he heard a noise coming from the direction of the tree-fort. Probably just a squirrel skittering through the maple branches. But some instinct urged him to double-check. He walked over and began climbing the ladder to the fort. He stuck his head through the opening in the floor. The fort was a platform with three walls. The fourth side was open to the lane but well camouflaged by branches. Nevertheless, one would be able, should one wish, to part the branches and have a commanding view of the lane. Stevie would be able to see his "enemies" coming. Garrett decided to climb onto the platform. In the rear wall there was a small, paneless window. Something made Garrett stick his head through. He looked down on a ledge protruding beyond the rear wall.

"Hello, Stevie," he said to the boy, who lay on the ledge reading a book. "The jig is up."

Garrett stood in the kitchen of the Shaw house while Susan gave Stevie a thorough scolding in the adjoining room. Her voice had as much exasperation as anger in it. The boy took his licks silently.

"Don't be too hard on him," he heard Uncle Wilbur say.

"It's his third time this month. And you know what that means, don't you?"

Stevie began to cry.

Susan came into the kitchen, her own eyes red and her face showing the strain of the past hour and a half. "The little bugger heard me calling him at the fort before you came, and never a peep out of him. It's the defiance and wilfulness I'm most concerned about. I'm at my wits end."

"You've tried corporal punishment?"

Susan's head snapped up. "I don't believe in that nonsense. The boy will stay in his room for the week. That'll be punishment enough for a lad who thinks that fort is his real home."

"I'm inclined to agree with you. My parents never laid a hand on me."

Susan looked surprised. "I thought you – being a policeman and all – would approve of a sound whipping for errant boys."

"As a last resort perhaps. But Stevie's not a bad lad."

Susan stared long and hard. "No, he's not," she said at last. "And that makes everything worse in a way."

"He'll be strapped at school?"

"My God, yes!" A new kind of anger filled her face. "That sadist Fagan will give him half a dozen on each hand. A ten-year-old in grade five!"

"That may stop the truancy, but it won't do Stevie much good in the long run, will it?"

"No, it won't. The boy misses his father and hates him at the same time."

"They were close?"

Susan appeared to be thinking about this. "I'd like to say that they were. The boy worshipped him, but Mike – well, Mike was . . . preoccupied. Being out of work for three years will do horrible things to even the kindest of individuals."

"I hate to see the lad strapped."

Susan smiled grimly. "I suppose there is nothing you could do, is there?"

Garrett hesitated, then heard himself say, "I could take Stevie back to school and have a word with principal Fagan."

Susan burst into tears. "Oh, would you, Stan?"

The principal – Bruce Fagan (known affectionately as "Brute" Fagan by many of his charges) – greeted them at the door of his office. On route, Garrett had had a brief conversation with Stevie.

"You know, son, that Mr. Fagan may strap you for playing hooky three times."

Stevie, his tears threatening to break out again, said, "Three times and out is what my pals say."

"So why do you persist? You don't want the strap, do you?"

"No, sir. I don't know why I ran off. Something just comes over me and I do."

"If I do you a big favour, would you make a solemn promise not to play hooky again?"

"What sort of favour?"

"I'm going to try and convince Mr. Fagan not to strap you. But only if I get that promise."

"But what if the feeling comes over me again?"

Garrett admired the boy for not leaping at the chance to make a promise he might not be able to keep. After a pause, he said, "When that feeling comes over you, I want you to come over to my house and talk to me."

Davie looked skeptical. "But you're a policeman."

"I'm also a friend of your mother's. And she would like it very much if we could solve this hooky business."

"You got any cards at your house?"

"I have. And a chess set. Would you like to learn chess?"

"You got a gun?"

"A revolver, yes. I'll let you see it, but nobody's allowed to touch it."

"That's super."

"Also, try to keep the feeling away until you get to your fort. I've even got a sleeping bag you could use if you wanted to sleep out there on cool nights."

"You've got a lot of things."

"So, do I get that promise?"

"All right."

"Let's shake hands on it."

Principal Fagan did not look happy. He frowned at Garrett and he frowned more strenuously at little Stevie, whose hand trembled in Garrett's.

"Stevie, you wait outside my door until I call you in. You are aware of the punishment you deserve?"

"He is," Garrett said.

"I believe the boy has a tongue in his head."

Fagan was a small, effeminate man with long, slim fingers and a pale face dominated by a pair of mean green eyes – squeezed tight like a cat's.

"I do, sir," Davie quavered. He let go of Garrett's hand and slipped outside.

"Thank you for returning the truant," Fagan said coldly. "Now if you don't mind, I'd like to administer the boy's punishment."

Fagan appeared as if he were looking forward to the event.

"I'm afraid I do mind."

Fagan blinked. "What do you mean? This is none of your affair. You've done your duty, sir."

Garrett decided a little creative lying was in order. "The boy is without a father. Mrs. Shaw has asked me to look out for the lad, to be a sort of role model for him."

"A policeman?" Fagan gasped, as if he had said "grave robber."

"Someone to look up to. A figure of authority."

Garrett's six-foot frame towered over the diminutive principal.

"Then as such, you should know the value of a good strapping. Spare the rod, eh?" Fagan was forced to take a step backward as Garrett edged farther into the room. The principal's voice had lost some of its snap.

"I have a nightstick and a revolver, sir, but I would use them only when reason and good sense no longer prevailed." Garrett stared into the green cat's eyes.

"The boy has shown no sense at all. And little remorse. He's had his warnings."

"He has promised me that he will not offend again, and I have every reason, sir, to believe him. He's not a bad lad, merely a troubled one."

"Rules are rules," Fagan spluttered, backed up against his desk. A school strap lay conspicuously across his blotter.

"To be broken with discretion," Garrett said. "I'm giving you my word that Stevie won't re-offend. If he does, then you may go ahead and apply your rules. What have you got to lose?"

"The pupils will be expecting – "

"Are you suggesting that your pupils will question your authority?"

Fagan was taken aback by the cold logic of Garrett's remarks. "All right, then," he said, straightening up to his full five-foot-five. "But I'll be forced to apply double the strokes on each hand."

"I assure you, you will not have to do so," Garrett said, hoping that his reading of Stevie was accurate.

"Good day, to you, sir."

Garrett backed out, patted a trembling Davie on the head, and then stood near the doorway until he heard Fagan say petulantly, "Go back to Miss Stevens, right this minute!"

Garrett left, shaking a little himself.

Garrett was grateful – and surprised – when nothing untoward happened on his afternoon patrol. He did spot Sideways Slim slinking along the wall of the Regency Arms, and flashed him a smile. He wasn't certain but he thought he got a shy grin in return. He also spotted Davie Shaw walking home from school – alone. He fell into step beside the boy.

"I didn't get the strap," Davie said.

"I know. And you'll keep your promise, eh?"

"I will."

"I heard you and your Uncle Wilbur had a little trouble fixing your bicycle the other day."

"A little. The rotten old thing won't go back together. I need a bike to go riding with the other fellas after school."

"How be I come over Saturday morning and take a look at it for you. I'm pretty handy with a bicycle wrench."

"Would you?"

"I'll be there at ten o'clock, after my morning patrol."

Davie thanked him and dashed off towards home, probably to stare at his bicycle and dream it whole again.

Garrett's evening patrol was also without incident. Breezy Harker stopped him on the street and said there were rumours flying that the City was planning to bring in a ringer from Toronto and pass him off as a local. Garrett promised to be extra vigilant on Saturday. He stopped in for a ginger-ale float at Maud's dairy-bar, and told her about the events of his first three days, hinting that he had begun to feel as if he had been here for three months. She assured him that there was no way to live in Port Eddy and not be involved in the minutiae of its daily life.

"You won't have as much time for your Agatha Christie as you may think," was her summary comment.

That evening he did get two more chapters completed before the phone rang. He picked it up.

"B-b-burglars!"

# CHAPTER 5

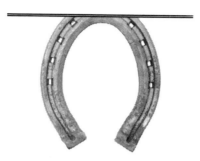

Prudence Shannon was too distraught to make tea. It took all her meagre store of courage to open the back door to Garrett.

"I did see him – again," she said when her breath returned for a short visit.

"Outside your sewing-room window?"

"Yes. He didn't look in, though. He seemed to be creeping along the back of my house, planning to do Lord knows what."

"What did he look like?"

Prudence paused, only partly to get her breath. "Hard to say. He was wearing a – a fedora, and dark clothes."

"A fedora? That's a strange thing for a sneak thief to wear."

"Could he be a peeping Tom?" Prudence's eyes ballooned at the thought, and a cold shiver ran down her spine. She needed a cup of tea.

"Possibly. Anyway, I'll check outside to see if I can spot any footprints." He really didn't expect to find any, but the poor woman was certainly spooked and had seen, or thought she had seen, something.

"I just turned over the flower bed below the window, Constable. This afternoon. The soil should be quite loose."

"I'll go and have a look – if you'll be all right here for a moment."

Prudence smiled. "I'll put on the kettle."

Garrett went outside and around to the sewing-room window. He shone his flashlight across the soft earth below it. There were fresh footprints, aimed towards the corner of the house a few feet away. They were large and definitely male. And they were very close to the house, which suggested that someone was indeed skulking beside the rear wall and not walking casually, say, from Prudence's back porch through the break in the hedge that led to the Turnidge place next door. Garrett looked farther afield but found nothing of interest. He went back inside.

Prudence was just making the tea. A plate of cookies was already on the table.

Half an hour later, Garrett – tea-laden – left Prudence's and walked through the gap in the hedge to Wilma Turnidge's house. There were no lights on. He rapped softly on the back door, just in case. But no-one answered.

Quite weary after such a long day, he was happy to go home to a warm, if lonely, bed.

Saturday turned out to be a glorious late-summer day. After a cool, clear September night, the sun shone brightly all morning, and by the time the County Horseshoe Championship was set to get under way, it felt like mid-July. The match was to be played at the Racetrack and Fair Grounds that sat at the south-eastern edge of the village. Lovingly groomed pits had been dug in the track below the grandstand, which was almost full by two o'clock. There were at least three hundred people from Port Eddy and an equal, if less vociferous, number from Petroleum City, each group sitting in its own jealously guarded section. At one end of the grandstand a concession booth had been set up, and was doing a brisk business in cold drinks, chocolate bars, ice cream and the like. Silverwoods Dairy had set up a small booth next to the larger one, and were doling out one free ice-cream cone to each child under twelve. Davie Shaw was seen lining up a second time with ice cream smeared on his cheeks and a different cap. The atmosphere was festive and electric with anticipation.

Precisely at two o'clock, Reeve Breezy Harker and Mayor Portland Gage led their delegations to the area between the two pits. While nothing could be heard, the crowd well knew what was taking place. The officials were being introduced and the formality of checking the bona fides of the four tossers was being carried out.

"Mr. Reeve," said the Mayor, "our official for this match will be Mr. Charles Derbyshire." He nodded to the man standing beside him. Derbyshire, known as Bull to his friends and enemies alike, was a big man whose large head, thick shoulders and heavy torso – combined with his small hips and spindly legs – made him look alarmingly like an American bison. His robust eyebrows, thrusting cheeks and beady brown eyes merely added credence to the illusion. He had been chief of detectives in the City police for over ten years.

"And our official," the Reeve said, "is Constable Stan Garrett."

Garrett and Derbyshire shook hands, each clasping tightly, as if they were commencing an arm-wrestling bout. Derbyshire stared into Garrett's face to let him know who outranked whom. Garrett stared back. He hoped that he would not be called upon to make any controversial decisions.

"Glad to me ya," Bull said, releasing his grip slowly.

"Likewise," Garrett said.

"You must be the fella takin' dear old Franny's place?"

"I'm going to try."

"I liked Franny," Bull said, indicating that the jury was still out on his successor.

"Mr. Derbyshire will supervise the south pit, Mr. Garrett the north," said Portland Gage, mayor of all the people. "Agreed?"

"We had the south last year," Breezy said, "so – yes, agreed."

"Now to the more significant matter," the Mayor said.

"The bona fides, yes."

"You will note that we have a new face on our team?"

"We have noted so."

"His name is Ray Stanton. He is a former City champion. Twenty years ago. He has decided to throw his hat in the ring, so to speak. And he has been a lifelong resident of the City."

"You have his address?"

"Yes. It's 211 Maxville Street. Here is the reference in this year's Directory."

Breezy made a great show of looking into the Directory, where dozens of names and telephone numbers jumped up at him in a dizzying daze. He thought he saw Ray Stanton among them.

"And he has happily supplied his birth registration," the Mayor said, brandishing a rumpled sheet of paper.

Breezy took it and called Garrett over.

"Looks legit to me. What do you think, Constable?"

Garrett saw that the paper was a standard birth registration form on the letterhead of the City Memorial Hospital. The name, scrawled in handwritten ink, was "Ray Stanton."

"And this is Mr. Stanton here?" Garrett said, nodding towards the fellow standing beside Tug Mason, the City's perennial tosser.

"It is."

"How come we haven't heard of him before now?" Breezy said. "We were expecting Tug and either Bolt or Lester. Like last year."

"Come out of retirement," the Mayor said smoothly. "Just for this occasion."

Breezy called Uncle Wilbur over. "You been watching these matches for many years, Wilbur. This fella is supposed to have won the City championship twenty years ago. Do you remember a Ray Stanton?"

"I do," Uncle Wilbur said. "A real wizard with a shoe. Just a kid." He peered over at Stanton, who smiled cryptically but said nothing. "Yes, that's the fellow all right. A little heavier, but it's him. I never forget a face."

"Then I guess we're all set to start," the Reeve chortled. "You know our two fellas, Harold Cooper and Clem Murphy, of course."

"How could one forget them?" the Mayor said with just a soupçon of bitterness.

The introductory proceedings were over. It was time to start the match. Garrett walked down to the north pit and stood beside the two tossers, in this case Tug Mason and Clem Murphy. The other two opponents walked with Bull Derbyshire down to the south pit. Bull flipped a coin, and the City team won the toss. The game was on.

The newcomer, Ray Stanton, tossed a ringer that clunked with authority and stuck to the post as if it had been magnetized. Harold Cooper took a deep breath and threw. His shoe revolved nicely and struck the post square, bouncing back. Garrett stepped up and pronounced it a ringer – just. One section of the crowd cheered. The other was silent. But before the cheers had died down, Stanton had rung the bell again. It was going to be that kind of a match. On the first throws, Stanton had tossed two ringers and Murphy a ringer and a leaner. The City squad had scored first, prompting a raucous cheer from the City section.

Garrett looked up and saw Susan Shaw and Uncle Wilbur in the front row, with Davie beside them, his face smeared with ice cream. The Shaw family had been given VIP seats.

Susan waved.

Archie Bolt and Matt Lester, the two tossers who had been beaten by the upstart Stanton, heard the cheer but did not see the action that had given rise to it. They were sitting on a straw-bale behind the horse-barn that stood to the north of the grandstand and the parking lot – a twenty-sixer of rye in hand.

"Maybe the bugger'll get his ass kicked," Bolt said, opening the bottle with a vicious twist.

"It ain't fair, is it?" Lester said. "The guy could've had one lucky night. We worked our way up the ladder, takin' on all comers and gettin' to the final against each other."

"And if he wins, there goes our hundred bucks." Bolt took a swig and passed the bottle.

Another cheer went up, the village one this time. You could tell because it was variegated: women, men and many children. The City cheer was more masculine, more adult, more intimidating.

"The villagers have scored," Bolt said. "Good."

"Better to lose and take a run at the hundred bucks next year," Lester reasoned, assisting his reason with a deep slug of whiskey.

"Still," Bolt said, "I'd like to rearrange that bastard's face. Just to teach him to go through the proper channels."

"It's the Mayor's fault," complained Lester. "Under that fancy dress, he's a sewer rat."

"And that so-called secretary of his hasn't seen the business end of a pencil since she was in kindergarten."

Another roar. Masculine this time.

"Christ, he's done it again," Lester moaned, reaching for the bottle. "You think he could be a ringer?"

"Hard to figure, ain't it? The guy's face is known. But for a fella to go twenty years without competin' and then suddenly appear like he did throwin' darts on the bull's butt – well, that's hard to figure too."

"I think we oughta shake him down, if we win. Make him give us a share of the loot." Lester, small and non-combative, was feeling his oats, whiskey-enhanced. Besides, Bolt was strong and tough. He took no guff from anybody.

"Good idea, Matthew. Let's plan to have a wee talk with the fella in the parkin' lot after the match – should he be as good as he thinks he is."

Another City roar of approval.

"He's good all right."

The City won the doubles match by six points. Ray Stanton threw all ringers but two, and one of them was a leaner. Poor Harold Cooper won only one point for his team, while Clem Murphy at the other end managed to keep the game close by tossing the game of his life against Tug Mason. Tug was not pleased at being upstaged by Ray Stanton, but was consoled by the thought of that hundred dollars promised to him as part of the winning squad, however much he was now playing second fiddle. Ray Stanton was indeed amazing, and the City folks began chanting his name as the first victory was sealed. The Port Eddyans put on a brave front, mustering a faint cheer in response. Both sides were soon drowned out as the pipe band from the village of Forest arrived and began skirling in earnest. They marched up and down the track, trailed by a dozen ragamuffins from both camps. One of the boys pretended to trip near the big drummer in the rear in order to get a peek under the man's kilt. But he landed on an elbow and squealed at the pain – abandoning his quest.

The next match was to be a singles contest between Tug Mason and Harold Cooper. Each side had decided to hold its ace back, should a third and deciding match be necessary. Thus, hope continued to spring eternal among the villagers. More ice cream was consumed, despite the five-cent price tag. Uncle Wilbur sought out Garrett at the edge of the grandstand. Amid the skirl of pipes he said:

"I can't believe anyone could throw like that without being competitive for twenty years."

"He is unbelievable. But you saw those ringers, one after the other. It made my job easy," Garrett said evenly.

"He sure looks like the Ray Stanton I saw all them years ago."

"You're not suggesting he's a ringer, from out of town?"

"Portland Gage would sell his own grandmother for a quarter," Uncle Wilbur said. "I suspect he's just taken the information given him and not bothered to double-check on it."

"But it's you we're relying on to verify who he is," Garrett pointed out.

"I just remembered something that might help. There was a story going around at the time that Ray had got into a dust-up with his brother and received a stick-wound. He was supposed to have a scar on the left side of his neck."

"And you think it might still be there, after all these years."

"Scars don't go away."

"True, but they do fade."

"Still, I'd like to get a peek at his neck."

"And how are we going to do that? We've had our chance to question the claims made for him. If the City squad wins, it will look like poor sportsmanship if we demand the fellow roll down his collar so we can look for a scar that may have faded anyway."

"I'll be with our group at the closing ceremonies," Uncle Wilbur insisted, "and I'll just sidle up behind him and have a gander."

"Even if we win?"

"That looks doubtful, doesn't it?"

Garrett had to agree. Anyway, if the village lost the second round, it would all be over and they could hardly blame a possible ringer for affecting a match he wasn't in.

The first singles match was a hard-fought and drawn-out affair. Both Tug Mason and Harold Cooper were at their best. The spectators were exhausted from cheering and sighing. but they were also aware that they might have to keep something in reserve for a possible deciding match. That possibility became a certainty when Tug Mason's shoe flew half an inch over the post and landed out of range, giving Cooper a narrow, two-point victory. The band, technically neutral, struck up a spirited march tune.

Out behind the horse-barn, two non-spectators were feeling no pain.

So it was all come down to a third match, pitting the wonder man against Clem Murphy, the village postmaster. Garrett was stationed again at the north pit, detective Derbyshire at the south pit. So far neither had had to make any crucial measurements. Garrett certainly was happy with that, happy to be able to cheer silently.

The game began with the players throwing south to north. They matched ringers. The crowd was oohing and aahing, but otherwise too concentrated on each toss to interrupt them with sustained cheers. Then both players missed, their shoes spinning away from the post. Both, however, were close enough for a measurement.

Garrett came out and lifted a shoe off the ring to use as a crude measuring stick. He had a tape in his pocket if a more refined one was needed. Bull Derbyshire strode from his south position to view the measurement. Garrett spanned the City shoe first, indicating the spot on the measuring shoe that he felt indicated the distance between the thrown shoe and the post. Derbyshire muttered his approval. Garrett repeated the procedure. The Port Eddy shoe was a good half-inch closer.

"Port Eddy's point?" Garrett said.

"Do it again," Derbyshire snapped.

"All right, if you insist," Garrett said, annoyed but not worried. He did the measurements again. The difference was palpable.

"Your point, then" Derbyshire grumbled. "This time."

Port Eddy had won a point on the first end! Hope surged through its fans. Ray Stanton was mortal! Perhaps the years of not playing had begun to affect his concentration. Certainly the pressure was enormous. He, like most others in the City, could use a hundred dollars, however illicit it might be.

The players walked down to Garrett's end.

"Good work," Murphy said to Garrett.

"I just measured, you threw," Garrett said.

Having found one chink in Stanton's armour, Clem Murphy continued to exploit others. The game see-sawed back and forth, with never more than two points separating the two contestants. The crowd had given up reacting in volume: prayerful oohs of approval and aahs of disappointment were all that could be heard. The county championship was heading for the final toss of the match.

With the score tied 20-20, the players, throwing to Derbyshire's pit, matched ringers. Then incredibly both players missed, their shoes banging off the post and coming to rest nearby. A hush fell over the crowd. This match could be determined by a measurement! Garrett walked down to oversee Derbyshire carry out this critical manoeuvre.

An anticipatory buzz, very faint – like the muttering of a communal prayer in the congregation – rippled through those gathered in the stands. Mayor Gage was seated in one of the front-row boxes. "This is it, Mildred," he whispered to his secretary, "My lifelong dream to have that trophy handed to me by Breezy Harker."

"Yes, Portie. I know. But you're sure our man ain't a ringer?"

The Mayor blanched. "I didn't go to his home and ask for a blood test," he snapped, "if that's what you mean. But he's been approved."

"But if he turns out to be a fake later, we'll still forfeit the prize."

"Christ, yes, and lose our two hundred dollars to boot. It'll be spent before we can blink."

"Well, let's just hope this measurement goes in our favour. First things first."

"We've got Bull doing the honours," the Mayor said with conviction. Then he reddened and said, "If that bugger is a ringer, I'll wring his neck for him."

Meanwhile, Bull Derbyshire had pulled out his tape measure, indicating to the hushed spectators that the shoes were too close for a rough measure. As Garrett peered over his shoulder, Bull leaned down and brushed dirt away from the Port Eddy shoe.

"I think you accidentally moved it," Garrett said quietly.

"What'd you say?" Bull growled, turning his massive head partway around.

"I said when you brushed the dirt away with your fingers, you accidentally nudged our shoe away from the post."

Bull stood up. His dark eyes blazed and his jowls shuddered. "Are you accusin' me, a police detective, of cheatin'?"

The crowd went eerily quiet.

"Not at all, I just thought I saw our shoe move."

"It was dirt, that's all."

"Very well," Garrett said, realizing there was no-one neutral to adjudicate.

"You've got a lot of nerve, just the same, a mere village flatfoot callin' my behaviour into question. I've been officiatin' at events like this for years!"

"Calm down, sir. And make your measurements. The people are waiting. As are the players."

"What's the hold-up?" boomed Mayor Portland Gage with all the authority vested in him.

"All right," Bull said. "But I ain't gonna forget this little incident." He bent over and measured the each of the shoe's distance from the post – twice. The City shoe was a quarter of an inch closer than the Port Eddy one – the distance Bull

Derbyshire may have nudged the latter. Bull stood up like a bison among his harem. "I declare Ray Stanton the winner of the game and Petroleum City the winner of the match, two games to one."

Wild, unleashed joy amid catastrophic disappointment. A quarter-inch had determined the result. Who could have predicted it? And Ray Stanton, though less than miraculous, was still the man of the hour, a hero for the ages.

Garrett was not absolutely certain of what he had seen, and Derbyshire's denials had been adamant. He felt he could not in all honesty lodge a protest. For him, not yet a true-blue villager and a man gainfully employed, this was just a horseshoe match. He would find out in the days ahead just how much the loss meant to the long-time citizens of Port Eddy in their historical struggle with the encroaching and rapacious City.

It fell to Breezy Harker's lot to present the County trophy to Mayor Gage, the polished silver cup that had been displayed on a conspicuous shelf in the village library, where everyone who arrived for a book was apt to pause and stare at it as if it were some sort of religious icon. A presentation platform was hastily dragged between the pits, while the band played lustily in a effort to hold the audience in place. However, the villagers were too stunned to move and the city folk were certainly not going to miss seeing the trophy change hands.

For Port Eddy, the Reeve, the two tossers and Wilbur Bright mounted the stand. For the City, the Mayor, his blond amanuensis, and the two City tossers mounted from the other side. In the middle stood the chairman of the Western Ontario Regional Horseshoe Association, Mr. Mowbray

Jenkins. On either side of the platform, like an honour guard, stood Constable Garrett and Detective Derbyshire.

The band struck up God Save the King, and some on the winning side felt compelled to sing along. Following the anthem, Mowbray Jenkins said a few words in as many words as he could summon up. The trophy sat on a stool just behind him. All eyes were upon it. At a silent signal, Breezy Harker moved over slowly and disconsolately to the stool and picked up the trophy. To sudden and thunderous (if lop-sided) applause, Breezy handed the gleaming cup to his counterpart, Portland Gage. He in turn raised it above him like the head of a dethroned lion. He directed Tug Mason and Ray Stanton to step over and bless it. The applause quickened, and some of it came grudgingly from the Port Eddy fans, who at least knew good tossing when they saw it – however bitter the results.

At this point, Uncle Wilbur stepped softly up behind Ray Stanton, and stared at his neck, visible in the open-necked shirt he was wearing. Over the strains of "For He's a Jolly Good Fellow," aimed at the City tossers, Uncle Wilbur cried, "Stop the proceedings! We have a fraud on our hands!"

The Mayor wheeled around and glared. "What the devil do you mean interrupting our show?"

"Your star player is a fake! This fellow is not Ray Stanton," Uncle Wilbur shouted as the band reached the climax of the old tune.

"Are you insane!" The Mayor was apoplectic. He looked from Uncle Wilbur to Ray Stanton.

"The old guy's nuts," Stanton said. His brown hair was slicked back and his shirt looked as if it had just emerged from the tailor's cutting table. It was hard to believe he had just spent over an hour in the hot sun pitching horseshoes. "I'm Ray Stanton and have been for thirty-six years."

"I thought you said you recognized him," Breezy Harker said sternly to Uncle Wilbur. "Have you changed your mind?" He almost added, "you befuddled old man," for the fellow was embarrassing him before his betters, whose support he would need when the next Tory provincial nomination meeting took place later in the year.

"The Ray Stanton I knew had a scar on the left side of his neck," Uncle Wilbur persisted. "And there's no sign of any scar on this man. He's a look-alike and no doubt an illegal ringer!"

Stanton laughed. "That old scar vanished years ago. It was never really very deep."

"There," said the Mayor with a prayerful glance at his secretary, "that clears the matter up. Now could we get back to the celebrations." He looked about. "Where in hell is the photographer from the Reporter? He's not here!"

"He's a ringer, I tell you," Uncle Wilbur shouted. "And I'm gonna prove it!"

"Constable, remove this man," the Mayor ordered Garrett.

Breezy nodded, and Garrett touched Uncle Wilbur on the elbow. "Perhaps you should step down, sir. You can pursue the matter later."

"It'll be too late, then. They'll cover it up. This man is not Ray Stanton."

"Look, your niece and her boy are waiting for you. Please, don't embarrass them."

"Let me go!" Uncle Wilbur cried, his face flushed with anger. He jerked away from Garrett and stomped off past the grandstand and past a startled Susan and Davie.

"Where in hell's that photographer? Nobody move till he comes!" the Mayor was hollering. The crowd had started to move off.

"I've got to hit the john," Stanton said. "I'll only be a minute." He stepped off the platform, walked past the north pit, and stooped down to pick up a horseshoe, a souvenir of his triumph. Then he sprinted towards the men's washroom, which was under the north side of the stands.

The Mayor's companion spotted the photographer coming across the open field to the south. "Here he comes, Portie."

"We'll need a picture of everyone around the trophy," the Mayor said, "just like they do with the Stanley Cup. Nobody move!"

The photographer came up and began, without apology, to set his camera on a tripod. A few hundred fans remained. The band had given up.

"Now where in blazes is Stanton?" the Mayor said.

"I'll fetch him," Tug Mason said.

"And where's Bolt and Lester? They can't be that miffed, can they?"

(Bolt and Lester were still behind the barn, much the worse for their afternoon's wear. In fact, Lester was out cold and snoring. Bolt checked to see that he was comatose, then slipped away. . . )

"I'll fetch him myself," the Mayor said. "I intend to give him proper hell." And he stomped off.

"This is turning into a fiasco," Derbyshire said five minutes later when neither the Mayor nor Stanton had returned.

"I'd better go and have a look," Tug Mason said.

The photographer was threatening to mutiny. Mason set off.

A minute later he returned, running.

"Constable, you'd better come. Something terrible's happened!"

Without further word, Garrett – trailed by Derbyshire and half a dozen others – followed Mason around the north end of the grandstand. As they did so, Mayor Gage emerged from the men's, hitching up his pants.

"What's going on?" he said. "I got caught short – "

Mason and Garrett swept by him. Just beyond the horse-barn, Garrett could see two fancy sedans, Chryslers by the look of them, parked off to one side, well away from the public lot. Mason raced between them and pointed at the ground. His face was as white as a ghost.

"Th-there!" was all he could say.

On the ground lay Ray Stanton. His skull had been crushed by some fierce blow with a heavy object. That object lay beside him – a horseshoe, matted with hair and blood. Stanton's eyes were open but were not seeing anything.

"Jesus," Garrett breathed, "he's been killed."

"And I saw the old fellow scamperin' off towards Bayside Park," Mason said as Derbyshire, the Mayor and the others puffed up. "He looked as if he was bleedin' from the head."

"Then we've got ourselves a murder," Detective Derbyshire said. "And a murderer."

# CHAPTER 6

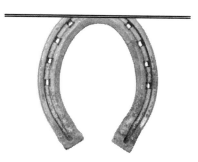

Bull Derbyshire swung into action. He pushed the gaping onlookers back, and ordered the Mayor to find a phone and call headquarters to report the incident. Then he turned to Garrett.

"I want you to see if you can pick up Wilbur Bright's blood trail and track him down. I'll have the village blocked off in half an hour, but you may be able to catch him before he gets clean away."

"But the crime was committed in Port Eddy," Garrett protested, not a little irked at Derbyshire's taking command.

"Tell him, Breezy," Bull said to the Reeve, who was straining to get a closer look at the body.

Breezy turned to Garrett. "We have an arrangement that in the case of serious crime we will turn over jurisdiction to the City police. They have the resources and the expertise."

"It's either us or the provincial police," Bull said, "and neither of us wants them."

"All right, then," Garrett said, and set off.

He picked up the trail of blood readily enough. Uncle Wilbur was bleeding, not profusely perhaps, but steadily. What had happened back there between those two Chryslers? Stanton had been felled with a vicious blow from a horseshoe, but the assailant, if it was Uncle Wilbur, was also wounded. Had there been a fight, ending in the fatal blow? But Uncle Wilbur was seventy years old. It was hard to conceive of him holding his own against a man like Stanton, let alone getting the best of him. But the old fellow had been close to rage back there on the platform, and rage did give a man strength. Moreover, that rage had been publicly directed at the victim. It certainly looked bad for Uncle Wilbur. Susan and Davie would be devastated.

Garrett followed the drops across the park road and into the park itself. There, in the thick grass, he lost them. But they were definitely pointed towards the marsh. Did the captain think he could hide out there? Or escape over the marsh to the docks? Garrett stood at the edge of the marsh, but could see nothing. Uncle Wilbur was gone.

Garrett returned to the scene of the crime, which was now crawling with City policemen and a scene of crimes crew.

"Got away, eh?" Derbyshire said, as if expecting the news.

"He's gone over the marsh towards the docks."

"We'll get him, then. I've got men watching all the exits to the village. Besides, he's an old man, and injured. How far can he get?"

"What can I do to help?"

"Just use your local knowledge to help us catch the fellow."

"I know his niece and great-nephew. I'll keep an eye on their house."

"That's exactly what I mean, Garrett."

Garrett paused before saying, "But what if the killer was not Captain Bright?"

Derbyshire looked as if he had just been told a joke without a punch-line. "Playin' detective now, are we? Don't be absurd. We've got two bloody men, one dead and one on the run. That's one plus one and it don't make three!"

"Stanton and Bright were in a fight of some sort, that's for sure. But someone could have happened along after Bright staggered off, hurt and confused. They could have picked up the horseshoe, and with Stanton himself down or dazed from the fight, decided to bash his skull in. Someone he knew, perhaps, whom he had no reason to fear, but who hated him."

"And who might that be?" Bull said contemptuously. "The man's been in seclusion for twenty years, he said. Where would he get enemies, except for you lot from the Port."

Garrett felt himself getting red in the face. "What about the two fellows I heard got beat out by him last week?"

"Bolt and Lester?"

"That's them. Where are they?"

"I don't give a damn where they are! They're a couple of losers. All they're good at doin' is whinin.'"

"All I'm saying, sir, is we should look around the scene for more evidence. And we should stop potential witnesses from leaving the scene."

"Act like a real detective, you mean?" Bull scoffed. "Stick to your bobbyin', eh?" And he turned to where the coroner was kneeling beside the body.

"What do you think, Sandy?" Bull asked him.

"One blow to the back of the skull. Instant death. Contusion on the cheek. Was probably struck there first."

"That jibes with what we figure," Bull said, much satisfied.

"It looks from here as if the fatal blow was struck while the poor chap was down on the ground. Felled there by the blow to the cheek perhaps."

"Keep that crowd back!" Derbyshire yelled to his minions. "Go and help them, Constable. Make yourself useful."

Garrett ignored him. Instead he went over to the big Chrysler, beside which the body lay. He looked carefully along the running-board. There was a smear of what looked like blood near the front door.

"Detective, there's a faint blood smear here."

Derbyshire came over. "Looks like it. I'll have it checked," he said stiffly. "But it don't mean bugger-all. There's blood on the grass and everywhere. These guys bled."

"I think he fell during the fight and struck his cheek on the running-board. Probably dazed him. He lies there on the ground and gets a horseshoe on the back of the skull."

"I'm ordering you to quit playing detective, Constable!"

"You can order me away from the crime scene, but this village is my territory, and I'll do as I see fit within its borders."

"Just stay the hell out of my way!" Bull seethed. "Last warning."

Garrett turned and walked away.

Garrett was worried about Susan and Davie, but he had his afternoon patrol to make, with a sharp eye out for Uncle Wilbur. The streets were near deserted, the village in mourning, not for the lost life of Ray Stanton (the news of which had just begun to hit the party phone-lines), but for the defeat at the hands of the City horseshoe squad. Breezy Harker came out of his empty shop to waylay Garrett.

"Any news?" he asked.

"Wilbur Bright is still missing," Garrett said, "and I'm sure the police are going to charge him with the murder of Ray Stanton."

"That's dreadful. You don't think the old fool did it, do you?"

"I don't think so, but we won't know till we hear his side of the story."

"Could Stanton have been a phony? A ringer?"

"Wilbur Bright certainly thought so."

Breezy sighed. "It would be great to launch a protest, but how can we? Wilbur claimed the real Stanton had a scar on his neck – at least that's what he told me before the presentation ceremony. But we can't very well ask the coroner to check for any trace of an old wound, now can we?"

"No, we can't. It looks as if the ringer business has died with Stanton. We'll never know."

A crafty look came over Breezy's face. "You wanted at one time to be a detective, didn't you?"

"I did, but that's in the past."

"Would you consider snooping about to see if you can find out whether Stanton is really Stanton? Play detective for us? If Stanton was a ringer, the trophy will return to us by default, and we can go on to the regional playdowns in London."

Garrett considered the request. "I could do that, as long as I keep well out of Detective Derbyshire's way."

"Good, good. Now let's hope we find Wilbur and he turns out to be innocent."

Garrett left Breezy and continued his rounds. As soon as he had finished, he went to Susan's house on Princess Street.

"Thank God you've come," Susan said at the door. "I'm worried sick. And Davie is beside himself."

"I came as soon as I could. But I haven't got any news. There's no sign of your uncle. The City police are combing the bush and the park."

"But they said he was hurt. My God, Stan, he's seventy years old! How far could he have got?"

"Not far. The police have an all-points bulletin out on him. And I intend to go out on the bicycle and search until it gets dark. But I had to see how you were faring first."

"The police are not interested in his health, are they?"

Garrett's face darkened. "I'm afraid not. Detective Derbyshire is certain that your uncle killed Ray Stanton in cold blood."

"That's crazy. He wouldn't harm a mosquito biting him."

"I believe you, but it's the police we'll have to convince."

"When we find him . . ."

Davie came into the room. He had been crying.

Garrett went over and put a hand on his shoulder. "Everything's going to be all right," he said. "Meantime you must try to be brave. Like your mom."

At this point they heard a stumbling noise at the back door. Susan ran and opened it. Uncle Wilbur staggered in.

When they had sat him down and put a cup of tea in his hand, Garrett said quietly, "Can you tell us what happened?"

Uncle Wilbur looked pale and anxious, but he was a sea-captain and not unused to difficult situations. The wound – a gash on his forehead – had been dressed somewhere between the marsh and home.

"At first I couldn't remember a thing," he said softly, and brushed away Susan's attempt to adjust the bandage. "Ray Stanton hit me with a horseshoe, and I was dizzy and damn near unconscious."

"But you did run off," said Garrett.

"I must have, but I barely remember. I guess I was in shock or something."

"I tracked you to the marsh. You bled quite a bit."

"It's just a graze on the scalp. Lots of blood but no permanent damage, I suspect."

"We'll have you checked by a doctor, just in case," Susan said.

"Who put the bandage on?" Garrett said.

"That's just it. I remember being on the marsh, but at that point I couldn't remember my name. Something drew me to the docks, and I found myself in the sailors' canteen. Some of my old cronies were there. They took me under wing. After a few minutes my memory started working again. But I was weak, and the fellas made me lie down. They assumed I'd fallen somewhere and cut my head."

"So you can now recall the incident behind the grandstand?"

"Parts of it, yes."

"What happened, Uncle? Did you and Stanton disagree?"

"Yes, Susan, I'm afraid we did. I was in a bit of a temper because I knew that fellow was an impostor. And he knew I knew. He was heading for the Mayor's car for some reason, and I trailed after him. We had words. I told him I was going to prove he was a fake. He laughed at first, then he got angry and pushed me away. I pushed him back. Then he just swung the horseshoe he had in his hand and clipped me on the forehead. I saw red and gave him a shove as I was staggering from the blow. He fell back, tripped and struck his face on the running-board of the big Chrysler. He was moaning. I don't remember anything after that until I found myself running through the marsh. I was, as I said, completely dazed. I didn't know who or where I was. I felt my feet moving but I had no idea where I was going."

"Till you reached the canteen and got help?"

"That's right." He took a sip of tea and looked into Susan's troubled face. "What's wrong? Stanton's all right, isn't he? He only hit his cheek on the car's running-board."

"Stanton's dead, sir. After you left, someone came along and killed him with his own horseshoe."

Susan blinked. "And the police are certain it was you."

Bull Derbyshire and two uniformed constables arrived to arrest Uncle Wilbur and take him down to police headquarters. Garrett stayed on to offer what comfort he could to Susan and Davie. It wasn't much.

"You'll need to get him a good lawyer, Susan. I believe he's telling us the truth. In fact I've suspected all along that his version is the true one, but Bull Derbyshire had already made up his mind. And certainly temporary amnesia, while possible, would not seem likely to someone like our chief detective. In his eyes, Uncle Wilbur had the motive and the opportunity. And a heavy iron horseshoe is a great equalizer."

"But I can't afford a lawyer."

"You may have to mortgage the house."

Susan grimaced. "That's already been done. Twice."

Bull Derbyshire sat across from Uncle Wilbur – a bare table between them – and stared hard at him with his beady, bison's eyes. Uncle Wilbur, used to commanding rough-and-ready seamen, stared back. And simply waited.

Bull blinked and said sharply, "Why don't you just confess and get this over with? It would save us all a lot of time and trouble."

"Confess to what?" Uncle Wilbur said. "Giving Ray Stanton, whoever he was, a push?"

"Don't be smart with me," Bull snarled, hunching his shoulders menacingly. "You know perfectly well what I mean. You crushed Ray Stanton's skull in with his own horseshoe. In a fit of rage."

"I did nothing of the sort."

"So he just hit himself on the back of the head, did he?"

"Stanton and I argued about his being a ringer, sir. He was the first to strike a blow. He clipped me on the forehead – here – with the horseshoe he had in his right hand."

"That's obvious, isn't it? But you managed to punch him one on the cheek, didn't you? A lucky blow for you because Stanton fell to the ground. And while he lay there, you viciously murdered him."

"He struck first, and I didn't punch him. I wouldn't have had the strength. I was dazed. I thought he was going to hit me a second time. So I just sort of lunged, almost fell against him. He tripped over backwards, spun around and struck his cheek on the Chrysler's running-board."

"You can hardly claim self-defence, can you?" Bull scoffed. "So he hit you first. What of it? A blow struck to the back of the skull does not suggest self-defence to me. Do you think we're stupid?"

"But I didn't deliver that blow, sir. I was dazed, befuddled. I don't remember anything after seeing Stanton fall and my staggering over the marsh. Even then, I couldn't even recall my own name."

"Oh, so now you're going to claim amnesia. How very convenient. But none of this will be of any importance once we find your fingerprints on that horseshoe, will it?"

"But I never touched the horseshoe!"

"We'll know soon enough. Meanwhile we've got you running away from the scene of the crime. Is that the action of an innocent man?"

"But I don't know why I ran, sir. I couldn't remem – "

"Ah yes. You had a convenient case of amnesia."

"I'm telling the truth, what I can remember of it."

"But if you can't remember what happened right after you pushed Stanton down, how do you know you didn't pick up that shoe and crush his skull?"

Uncle Wilbur looked momentarily stunned.

"And you see, Captain, I've got a wee problem, haven't I? I've got a bloody man fleein' the scene and a man dyin' of a head wound. If you didn't kill Stanton, how did he get his skull bashed in, eh? Our witness, Tug Mason, saw you runnin' towards the park. That means there was only a minute or less for someone to come along, spot the unconscious Stanton, do him in, and run off – without being seen by Tug Mason. Impossible, isn't it? So don't try giving me a cock and bull story about bein' befuddled and sufferin' from amnesia. I may have a thick skull, but I do have a brain."

"We were between the two big sedans. Someone could have seen us struggling and – in my daze I don't remember nor could I likely have seen that person – but he could have come right up behind me and killed Stanton. If Mason was looking over at me near the park, he might not have seen the killer skulking behind the cars. When Mason leaves to report the crime, the killer just slips away."

"Who's the detective here, eh?" Bull cried, thumping his fist on the table. "I ask the questions and I develop the theories. What you say is possible, but not probable, is it? It's as far fetched as an Agatha Christie novel. And we ain't in a novel, Captain."

"I just wish I could recall those few minutes between my being struck and walking on the marsh. But I can't."

"Then unless you do remember and can give us a description and the name of this phantom figure, I have no choice but to have you arraigned on a first degree murder charge."

For the first time Uncle Wilbur's composure failed him. He heaved a big sigh and hung his aching head wearily. He was thinking of Susan and little Davie.

Despite Bull Derbyshire's warning, Garrett was determined to find the real killer of Ray Stanton. He already had two suspects in mind: Archie Bolt and Matt Lester, the disaffected City tossers. Rumour had it, according to Breezy Harker, that there was money under the table for any City tosser beating Port Eddy, so jealousy and spite might be strong motives, if not for murder then for a little payback that got out of hand. With Stanton lying groggy beside the Chrysler, it would be tempting to give him a knock with the horseshoe – delivered in anger. Besides, the pair had been seen before the match started but not after. Where were they?

Of course Bull Derbyshire had let all the potential witnesses to any aspect of the crime go on their merry way. Garrett couldn't very well start interviewing villagers at random in the faint hope that someone had actually witnessed the incident. But he could start with Bolt and Lester, if he could find a way to question them without rousing their suspicions and having them report him to Bull Derbyshire.

He explained all this to Maud Marsden over a ginger-ale float on Monday afternoon. Wilbur had indeed been indicted and held in custody without bail. Susan was visiting him as Garrett was chatting with Maud.

"Lester and Bolt were seen by Breezy with a bottle of whiskey heading for the barn," Maud informed him. "That's only a few yards from where the two sedans were parked. If they didn't do it themselves, then they were certainly in a position to see who did."

"I tried to get Derbyshire to start questioning potential witnesses, but he felt he had his man. I got nowhere with an alternative theory."

"And, speaking of people with motives," Maud said, "what about Portland Gage?"

"The Mayor?" Garrett said, surprised. "What motive could he have?"

"Well, it's said he'd sell his soul – should he have one – to the devil or the highest bidder if he could be guaranteed possession of that trophy."

"But he got it," Garrett pointed out.

"True, but Wilbur Bright was threatening to expose a fraud, wasn't he?"

"I see, I think."

"What if Gage didn't know about Stanton perhaps being a ringer? When he heard Wilbur's accusation, he may have thought, "'Here we go again. Forfeiture and another lost opportunity to win that trophy.' He becomes enraged at Stanton. When he finds him dazed beside the Chrysler, he loses it and gives the fellow a pounding with the horseshoe."

"But he was in the men's room during the incident. He joined us on the way there."

"He led you to believe he was."

Garrett smiled. "I see what you're saying. The Mayor left the platform to look for Stanton. Perhaps he found him, killed him, and then beetled back to the men's room."

"Exactly."

"Damn Derbyshire. If we had stopped potential witnesses from leaving the grounds, we could have cleared this whole thing up in short order."

"True, but how to find witnesses without upsetting Mr. Derbyshire, who guards his territory like a mastiff."

"I can't very well advertise in the City paper, can I?"

"Well, you could ask Breezy to put out a discreet word. He sees the male half of the town in his shop."

"I can't imagine he'd be discreet, but it's worth a try."

"You could start yourself by talking – discreetly – to Bolt and Lester."

"I'll have to think up a good cover story."

"Somehow I don't see that as being a great hurdle."

Garrett finished his float, thanked Maud, and left, determined somehow to play detective.

Garrett spent the afternoon tidying up the house and finishing his Agatha Christie. About four o'clock the phone rang.

"Constable Garrett?"

"Speaking."

The voice on the line was female and tremulous. "I'd like to report a robbery."

"Miss Hannah?"

"Yes, this is Hannah Bristol."

"Have you been robbed personally?"

"It's my bike. Somebody took it from the side of the house."

"When do you think this happened?"

"Just a few minutes ago. I came back from a ride and parked it in its usual spot. I had a cup of tea and went back out to look at my garden and saw it was missing."

"I'll go right out and ride around myself.," Garrett said. "What kind of bike is it?"

"A ladies' CCM, but repainted green."

"Don't worry, we'll get it back."

Garrett rang off. He remembered that the rash of bicycle thefts had each ended with the bike being ridden and then abandoned. He thought of Davie Shaw, then dismissed the thought. He and Davie had spent Saturday morning repairing the boy's old CCM and making it rideable. The lad had not played hooky again and had been delighted with the bike. Garrett had got a lunch for his efforts and a long conversation with Susan (Uncle Wilbur blessedly absent). That seemed an age ago. Wilbur was now in jail and Susan in desperate straits.

He rode all over the village without sighting the culprit. As he was coming back from the docks, he spotted Max Barwise sitting on the stoop behind his pool hall, smoking. He wheeled up.

"Afternoon, Constable. You doing an extra patrol today? You're allowed some time off, you know."

"Another bike reported stolen. Miss Hannah's."

"Oh my, that's the second time for poor Miss Hannah." He stepped on his cigarette. "She'll be in a state. But I think it'll turn up. The last one was left in that field down there."

"Thanks. I'll come back and check the spot."

"Meantime, I'll keep my eyes peeled."

Garrett made another circuit of the village. Then he decided to camp out behind the pool room. It was supper hour and the village was unnaturally quiet. He planted himself in the alley between the pool hall and the Regency Arms. And waited.

He didn't have to wait long. He heard the whir of a bicycle speeding down Elizabeth Street, a block to the south. Seconds later it turned up the alley at a breakneck clip. The rider was Sideways Slim Coote. His dishevelled hair floated out behind him. His loose shirt flapped in the breeze made by his headlong haste. As he neared the rear of the pool room, Garrett could see on his face a look of sheer ecstasy. He removed his feet from the pedals and let the ladies' green bike coast to a stop in the grass at the edge of Barwise's property. He slid off backwards, letting the bike float out between his long legs. He heaved a big, satisfying sigh. Then everything changed. Suddenly he began jabbering and moved jerkily to the rear wall of the pool room. He slid along sideways with his back to it until he came to the far corner.

Garrett could see now that there was at the edge of the marsh, about a hundred yards away, a shack of sorts, that he had assumed was abandoned. Slim made a break for it, running zigzag and dodging shells, as fast as his long legs would carry him. He didn't stop till he reached it. He entered, and slammed the door shut.

Miss Hannah's bike, none the worse for wear, lay in the grass.

"I'm going to get him a used bike," Max Barwise said behind Garrett. "I've got a line on one. Hope to pick it up tomorrow."

"He feels safe on a bike?" Garrett said.

"Only on a bike, I'm afraid."

"I'll take this one back to Miss Hannah."

"He'll stop 'borrowing' as soon as he gets something of his own."

Garrett started walking both his bike and Miss Hannah's over to Duchess Street where the latter lived with her mother. He smiled to himself. There was no way that Max Barwise had not known all along who the bicycle thief was.

Sometime later that evening (with no frantic call from Prudence Shannon), he thought of exactly how he would approach Bolt and Lester. But before he did that, he felt obligated to see if he could find out more about Ray Stanton or whoever he had been. It seemed possible, likely even, that information gained in that quarter would help him with the investigation of the murder itself.

He had only an address to go on: 211 Maxville Street. It might be enough.

# CHAPTER 7

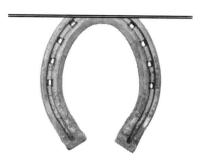

Before going to check out Ray Stanton's home address on Tuesday morning, Garrett thought he would have another look around the crime scene. Bull Derbyshire had been so certain he had his man that he had asked the scene of crimes people to scour only the immediate area. There had been blood drops everywhere, including the running-board of the Chrysler. But perhaps the real killer had left something else behind. Garrett ignored the police tape. It took him a little while to find the exact location where the two Chryslers had been, but their tire tracks were still visible in the soft grass. Garrett walked back and forth in a grid pattern about thirty yards on either side of the spot where the body had lain. He noted that anyone behind the horse-barn would not be able to see anything in this vicinity. But the public parking lot was only forty yards away. There had been few cars in it

– many cars were now up on blocks waiting for the depression to end – but folks leaving the match would walk across it to exit on the park road. The trouble was that the fight and murder had occurred between the two sedans, obscuring their view. Still, someone could have heard something or spotted someone besides Uncle Wilbur running off.

He was just about to give up – having found and discarded a dozen bits of irrelevant detritus – when he came across something that could be pertinent. A jackknife. Not rusted. Dropped here recently, perhaps on Saturday. It was an expensive bone-handle one, and was stamped with the letter "B." That could mean anything really, but might help to identify it eventually. He ought to show it to Derbyshire but he knew he would be greeted with contempt. He put the knife in his pocket.

He got back onto his bicycle and rode through Bayside Park until he reached Petroleum Drive, the city-village boundary. He had got instructions from Maud Marsden about how to find Maxville Street. It took him less than twenty minutes as the City's streets were laid out in a perfect grid pattern. He pedalled down to number 211. It was a modest cottage with a weed-filled front lawn and curtains drawn tight across the two front windows. The side walk was unswept and unwelcoming. Garrett decided to try the back door.

The back of the cottage was actually a wide, screened-in porch. The morning sun glanced off the blinds that covered every inch of the screen. He glanced around and noticed a horseshoe pitch, recently used. He rapped on the screen door. No answer. Several more raps did nothing to bring anyone to the door. Well, if Ray Stanton really was the owner of the house and its sole occupant, and was now dead, it stood to reason that no-one would be at home. But Stanton had a brother. Monday's front-page story of his triumph and tragedy had indicated a brother, Roy, who had moved away some years ago. He had obviously not yet been located or, if he had, had either not come for the funeral or had come and decided not to take advantage of the empty cottage. Still, since the paper said the Stanton parents were dead and Roy was the closest and nearest relative, this cottage would likely be his now.

"He's in there!"

The call came from the back yard next door. An elderly woman with a plump body and cherubic face said again, "He's always in there."

"Mr. Stanton?"

"That's right. Just look at the weeds in that yard. The seed blows over into mine and keeps me plenty busy. And I ain't getting any younger."

"But he doesn't answer."

"He will if he knows who you are. You gotta announce yourself."

"He's a recluse, then?"

"You could say that."

This was strange news. Could the brother have been living here all along? And if so, why was he not out finalizing the funeral arrangements? Garrett was about to ask this neighbour lady when she turned abruptly to go back into her house, where the phone was ringing.

He went back to the door of the cottage. He rapped and shouted, "I'm a friend of your brother!"

Some shuffling behind the blind on the screen door. It inched open.

"You want to see me?"

"I'm the Port Eddy constable. I was nearby when your brother was killed. I've come to offer my condolences." The lie seemed harmless enough. He had to be careful not to spook this fellow and have Derbyshire come down on him like a ton of bricks.

"All right, then. Do come in. I'm not unfriendly." He opened the door and motioned Garrett to follow him into the kitchen, where a freshly perked pot of coffee sat on the gas-range. "I'm not afraid of people, just open spaces."

"You suffer from a phobia?"

"I do. It's called agri-phobia or something. I don't go out-doors except for two or three steps into my garden.

As far as that well-used horseshoe pitch, Garrett won-dered. "And you are Roy Stanton, Ray's brother?"

Stanton nodded, very slightly. He was a thin, pale shadow of a man, who looked indeed as if he had spent his life indoors. Except for his thinness, however, he resembled his brother – with the same eyes and light brown hair and jutting chin.

"I understood you lived outside the City, some ways away?"

"I did, but I came back three months ago."

"You managed to travel?"

"I can ride in the back seat of a car with the blinds down."

"I see."

"Would you like a cup of coffee, Constable. I get few visitors."

"Yes, please."

Stanton served them two mugs of very delicious coffee.

"So you won't be able to attend the funeral?"

Stanton paled even more. "Oh, good gracious, no. The room in the funeral home would be too large for me – and all those people."

"How did you make the arrangements?"

"I didn't really. I called the funeral home and they said the City would conduct the funeral – they'd found a hero, I guess. I told them to go ahead."

"So you'll have to read about it in the paper?"

He nodded. "Did you see the actual murder?"

"No. I was only yards away, though. It was a vicious crime."

"And they've got the killer, thank God."

"You must have found your brother helpful, with your condition and all."

"He was. We weren't close, though. We'd gone our separate ways for many years. We only got back together three months ago."

"He could help with shopping and looking after the garden. I noticed one well-tended rosebush near the back door. And that horseshoe pitch is well looked after."

For the first time a sadness crept into Stanton's face. "Yes. That was my mother's rosebush. It's been the only thing cared for outdoors, except the pitch, which my brother loved more than himself."

Garrett was sure now. "The rosebush was kept up by you," he said quietly. "Not by your brother."

Stanton did not look up. "How did you know?" he said.

"You fitted perfectly into this house and the neglected yard. You moved about as if you'd lived here a long time, not three months. And your neighbour said you never left the house, as if that 'never' had been a long time."

"I'm ashamed of myself," he said, looking up, his face full of pain. "But once it got started I didn't know what to do to stop it."

"You are Ray Stanton, aren't you?"

"Yes." It was a whisper.

"Your brother Roy pretended to be you in order to be eligible for the horseshoe championship, didn't he?"

"Yes."

"Tell me about it."

"All right. I need to get this off my chest. And perhaps you'd be good enough to convey the truth to the Mayor and others."

"I'll do that for you, yes."

"As I said, Roy came back here three months ago. He lost his job in Etobicoke. He'd spent all his savings. He always was a free spender. Anyway, he knew I'd been living here in our mother's house for fifteen years, following her death. He'd at least have a roof over his head and could look for a job. And he was helpful to me. Then he got this bright idea of posing as me to enter the playdowns, as he was not eligible himself. He had been the Etobicoke champion three times, but had never played outside the Toronto area. I objected, but he said there was money to be made."

"How? It's an amateur championship."

"I don't know. But he said it would give him a stake, enough to get him back to Etobicoke and his cronies."

"And he used your birth registration and this address to make his case. You do look alike and no-one who mattered had seen you for many years. He must have also figured that your mayor would not ask too many difficult questions."

"He did not use my birth registration. It's over in that drawer."

"Then he must have changed the 'o' of Roy to the 'a' of Ray on his own. I saw it."

"That's what he did, right over there on the kitchen table."

"And he got lucky in that one of the old-timers from Port Eddy identified him as the Ray Stanton he'd seen twenty years ago."

"That happened at the City playdowns as well. He laughed about it. I did try to talk him out of it, you must believe me. Then when they called to say he was dead, they referred to me as Roy, and the papers were already full of Ray Stanton's triumph and tragedy."

"And those few people who know you would have assumed 'Ray' was a misprint or natural confusion."

"What could I do but go along with the charade?"

"You could have done what you've done with me – tell the truth."

"I know that now. I've been cowardly and stupid. And I don't really think I would have let it go on much longer. I've slept little since all this happened."

"Well, it was your brother who perpetrated the fraud. He took advantage of you and your illness."

"Will I be charged?"

Garrett considered this. "I don't believe so."

"I couldn't leave this house to go to court, could I?"

Garrett felt both proud and saddened. Proud that he had quickly exposed Roy Stanton as a fake and an illegal ringer. Saddened because he felt sorry for the handicapped brother, overwhelmed by the more aggressive man. He thought of riding home and informing Breezy Harker right away. But he wanted to talk to the Mayor before word about the fraud reached him from other sources.. He also needed a way to question the Mayor about the murder. He thought of one just as he pedalled up to City Hall and parked his bicycle in the racks at the side.

He made his way to the outer office, patrolled by the blond secretary.

"The Mayor is in conference, if that's who you're after," she said, pre-empting him.

"Please, tell him it's Constable Garrett and I have some disturbing news about the horseshoe competition and the awarding of the trophy."

She frowned, looking doubtful, but buzzed through and gave Portland Gage the message.

"You are to go right in," she said, still frowning.

The Mayor put down his putter and waved Garrett to a chair. Then he himself sat down opposite him across the desk.

"What sort of disturbing news?" he said, looking curious but not alarmed. The prize trophy stood on a plant-stand to the left of the desk, next to the Union Jack.

"I'm sorry to have to inform you, sir, that your champion tosser, Ray Stanton, was not who he claimed to be."

The Mayor's substantial jaw dropped. "What on earth do you mean? The fellow was vouched for by several of our veterans and your own manager."

"They were understandably mistaken, sir. The man claiming to be Ray Stanton was really his brother Roy. They look somewhat alike."

"That's preposterous!" The Mayor's brows shot up and down so violently they almost detached themselves. "You have proof of this absurdity?"

"I have his brother's word. He went along with the deception unwillingly, and is now prepared to tell all. I have his phone number here. He wishes to apologize to you personally."

"Apologize! Apologize!"

"He feels badly that he let his brother have his way. The fellow, who was from the Toronto area by the way, went so far as to forge a birth registration. I believe the attempted forgery will be evident when it's examined under a microscope."

"But we had no idea!" the Mayor spluttered. "The devil fooled us as well as everybody else."

"He was very clever and indeed a champion tosser in his home town."

"Breezy will seize on this to claim a forfeiture," Gage said with an anguished glance at the trophy, polished and gleaming on its stand.

"He has a right to."

"But we perpetrated no fraud. We are victims, too."

"I'll convey that sentiment to him, sir."

"Oh, would you? I'd be most grateful." He was grateful also, but decided not to say, that the two hundred dollars had not yet been doled out – to Tug Mason and to the reputed brother of the dead man.

"And I would be grateful, sir, if you would answer me a few questions about what happened Saturday."

Gage's gaze narrowed. "Why? You're not investigating, are you?"

"Oh, no, sir. Nothing like that. But the accused is claiming he was struck first, and therefore will be able to claim self-defence. Especially if he gets a smart lawyer, which rumour has it he intends to do."

Gage looked grim. "And get off Scot free?"

"I'm afraid it may be so."

"Stanton may have been a fraud, but he didn't deserve to die like that."

"And he threw a mean horseshoe, didn't he?"

Gage closed his eyes, picturing that delicately revolving shoe as it struck the post and nuzzled it. "That he did. But I don't see how I could help out with what happened. I've told Bull that I had to duck into the men's, and didn't see the fight."

"But if we could get some evidence of any sort that would help deflate the self-defence theory, we can be sure to convict Wilbur Bright."

"The meddling old fool. Thought he was God's gift to the sea."

"When you were at the door of the men's, you were only thirty or forty feet from those two Chryslers."

"True. I did hear something, but paid little attention."

"What was that?"

"Two men arguing. I couldn't see who because they were between the cars."

"Did you hear any words?"

"I did. One of them said, 'Lay off or I'll kill you!'"

"And you thought nothing of this?"

"A couple of drunks, I thought. They'll say just about anything."

"You didn't recognize the voice?"

"No, but the other one said, 'It's you that deserves to die.'"

Oh dear, Garrett thought. This is not what he came to hear. It sounded like an exchange of threats, each offering to kill the other. Bull would be certain to interpret it as if at least one of the threateners was his suspect – by logical deduction as no third person had yet been discovered. Doing his duty, however, Garrett said, "And you didn't tell this to Detective Derbyshire?"

"He only asked if I saw the fight. I said no. He didn't ask any more questions."

Hating himself for doing so, Garrett said "I think you ought to tell your story to Detective Derbyshire right away."

"And you'll tell Breezy the fraud had nothing to do with us?"

"I will." But you are not above giving your competitors money under the table, Garrett thought – a move he had no real evidence for, alas. He thanked Gage and left the man staring wistfully at the silver cup that had almost been his.

It was late Tuesday afternoon when Garrett, on his patrol, stopped in at the barber shop. Breezy had a single customer, an old gent that Garrett did not recognize.

"I've got news," he said to Breezy, and whispered, "For your ears only."

"Oh, don't worry about old Abner," Breezy said. "He's as deaf as a post, AIN'T YA, ABNER!" Abner didn't twitch.

So while Breezy clipped away, Garrett told him about his visit to the real Ray Stanton.

Breezy whistled through his teeth. "Well, don't that beat all. I always knew Portland Gage was a fraud. He'd cheat his own mother out of her pension."

"But I'm pretty sure he didn't know about the deception. At least he claims he didn't."

"Doesn't matter one way or another, does it? Rules are rules. The match is forfeited to us, and he'll have to return the trophy. Jesus, but I'd like to see his face!"

"It wasn't a pretty sight."

Breezy started lathering Abner's cheeks, preparatory to a shave.

"I'll go down to City Hall first thing in the morning. I'll close up the shop."

"Don't you think you should call the Council together to discuss the situation?"

"What for? What's to discuss?"

"Well, if Gage and the City folks were fooled by Stanton's deception, they can hardly be accused of deliberately using a ringer, can they?"

Breezy's little eyes narrowed. "Is that how you city people think things out?"

"It was just a suggestion. And if you had the Council behind you, your visit to City Hall in the morning would go a lot more smoothly."

Breezy grinned. "Why you sly old bugger. So it would. I'll send for the Council and we'll meet at the library at eight o'clock."

"I should be there to explain what happened in detail."

"So you should, Constable."

"And I may even take you to City Hall to make sure that trophy gets uprooted right and proper."

Abner flinched as Breezy nicked him.

"I'll leave you to your work," Garrett said.

At precisely ten minutes past eight the last of the councillors, Farley Joiner, arrived for the meeting. Already present were Breezy Harker, Max Barwise, Maud Marsden, Miss Hannah and, as special invitee, Constable Stan Garrett. With a pretty blush, Miss Hannah again thanked Garrett for returning her bicycle. And Barwise took Garrett aside and assured him he had been successful in securing a bike for Sideways Slim.

"You're adapting to our ways mighty quick," he said with a smile.

"I'm finding them pretty easy to adapt to," Garrett said truthfully. And he was very happy to able to say so.

"Now that we're all here," Breezy said with a glower at the latecomer, "this special session will begin."

"Rumour has it we could get the trophy back," Joiner said.

The glower deepened. "What rumour?" Had old Abner read lips in the barber shop's mirror?

"Would you like me to clear that up?" Garrett said with a wink at Maud Marsden.

"Yes, Constable," Breezy said, shuffling some papers before him. "I've invited the constable here for a special reason related to the horseshoe match and the trophy. Our constable has been doing some excellent detective work."

Garrett again summarized his meeting with the pathetic Ray Stanton. There was amazement around the table.

"So we were up against a ringer?" Barwise said.

"A very elaborate deception," Maud said. "You were diligent at ferreting out the truth, Constable."

"That bugger Gage is behind all this!" Joiner said, drawing a blush from Miss Hannah and a stutter of her pencil.

"As I told Reeve Harker earlier," Garrett said, "Portland Gage insisted on saying that he was duped as much as we were."

"Of course he'd say anything to keep the trophy," Breezy said.

"You're thinking we should not apply the rules strictly?" Maud said to Garrett.

Breezy glared at Maud, as if chastising her for having the nerve to speak, as if just tolerating her on the Council were proof of his vast good nature. "Rules are rules," he said, patting the papers in front of him. "And forfeiture of the match is the price for playing with an illegal contestant. It says so in black and white."

"But we ourselves verified Stanton, did we not?" Maud said, ignoring Breezy, which manoeuvre was sure to anger him more than any direct confrontation. "Wilbur Bright, poor soul, identified him for us and, tragically, changed his mind."

"We're not here to chatter about Wilbur, sad as his story is," Breezy said briskly. "We're here to get the trophy back where it belongs." He nodded at the vacant spot on a nearby shelf.

"What about that birth registration?" Joiner said.

"According to the real Ray Stanton, it was forged," Garrett said. "Which gives credence to the Mayor's claim that he was also duped. And several of the old-timers from the City also identified the impostor as legitimate."

"Oh, dear," Maud said. "It looks as if the Mayor does have a case."

"For what?" Breezy snarled.

"For extending them an invitation to a rematch," Barwise said. "It's the only honourable thing to do."

"The only honourable thing to do is get that trophy back!" Breezy said, giving the rules a cuff.

"I believe the proper procedure is to vote on the question," Maud said.

Breezy, red-faced, knew when to retreat. "All right, then. A vote it is."

By a margin of three to none – with one abstention – the motion to invite the City to a rematch this coming Saturday was passed.

On the way out of the meeting, Maud said to Garrett, "How is the other investigation getting on?"

"Well, I did take time to quiz the Mayor about what he saw and heard last Saturday."

"And?"

"And he heard what was probably the initial argument between Captain Bright and Roy Stanton. Unfortunately he heard threats on both sides."

"Oh, dear," Maud said, stepping onto the street. "Are you going to tell Detective Derbyshire?"

"Eventually, if Gage himself doesn't. Since Derbyshire's already charged the Captain, there's no hurry. I still hope to find the real killer before anything else becomes necessary."

"Where will you go next?"

"To Matt Lester and Archie Bolt."

"Good tossers, but a dubious pair, from all I've heard."

"They disappeared during the match, and I suspect did not go far. The real Ray Stanton hinted to me that a lot of money could have been at stake in the match for the City contestants. I think Lester or Bolt held a grudge that could have led to murder."

"Well, good luck."

"I hope I won't need any."

Maud stared at him. "No, somehow I don't think you will."

# CHAPTER 8

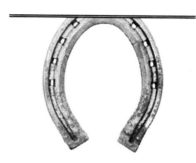

After his morning rounds on Wednesday Garrett pedalled all the way to the far side of the City to the lumber mill where both Bolt and Lester worked. Bolt worked in the shop itself, so he was easy enough to find. He was busy sorting two-by-fours at the far end of the barn-like building. The sight of Garrett's uniform turned a few heads, and he wished for once that he was a plainclothes detective. Bolt, a strong, heavy-set man, looked up not in surprise but in total indifference.

"Something I can help you with?" he said mechanically, turning back to his sorting.

"I've come to talk about what happened last Saturday."

"I thought Derbyshire had his man."

"He does. But it's a question of gathering enough evidence to make sure we convict the fellow. I thought I'd help out." This was a close as he felt he could go to saying he was actually investigating. He didn't want to spook either Bolt or Lester.

"As far as I'm concerned, you could give him a medal," Bolt snapped, banging one two-by-four on another.

"You didn't like your star tosser?" Garrett was tempted to tell him about the fraud, but he wanted Breezy and the Mayor to publicize it as they saw fit. Breezy, wishing to have the Mayor suffer a little longer, had delayed his visit to City Hall.

"He horned in at the last minute and got lucky," Bolt said.

"Nevertheless, the guilty must be convicted and punished."

"Nothin' to do with me, is it?" Bolt began piling wood.

"I was told you were seen in the vicinity of the crime," Garrett lied.

"Then you were told a whopper."

"We're hoping to get eye-witness accounts, that's all. Nothing here for you to worry about," Garrett said smoothly.

"Well, the closest I got to those two Chryslers was the back of the horse-barn. If you want to know, Matt and I got ourselves pie-eyed there on a quart of whiskey. We were feelin' mighty sorry for ourselves. And that's it."

"So you saw nothing?"

"That's right."

"Did you hear anything?"

"Just the gurgle of whiskey in the bottle."

"All right. Thanks for your time."

Garrett sensed the man was lying, but decided to have a go at Lester. He sounded, from Maud's description, the weaker of the two vessels.

Lester was in the yard, unloading a box car of barn-board, by the looks of it. He started when he saw the uniform.

"No need to worry, sir. I've just come to ask you a few questions about the tragic events last Saturday."

"I didn't do nothin'!" The little man's face was suddenly anxious.

"I'm not here to accuse you, sir. I'm hoping to help Detective Derbyshire find some eye-witnesses to the altercation between Wilbur Bright and Ray Stanton, as he called himself."

"I couldn't see a thing, Constable. I was blind drunk."

"When did you and Mr. Bolt go behind the barn?"

"Soon as the match started. We were disgusted with that ringer."

"So you just sat behind the bar and drank?"

"Yeah. Me and Archie. We been pals for years. And one of us should have been playin' with Tug, not Stanton."

"But surely you heard something? Stanton and Bright were arguing not twenty yards away."

"How could I? By the time all that fuss started, I was out cold."

Garrett was taken aback, but recovered quickly. "You passed out?"

"The match was still goin' on 'cause I could hear the cheers. Then it was lights out."

"So you can vouch for Archie Bolt's presence only until you passed out?"

"Well, I guess so. I ain't got no power of mental telegraphy."

Garrett thanked him and went looking for Bolt. He was certain now that Bolt had been in the area of the crime at the critical time – without an alibi. Bolt was not happy to see him.

"I thought you were lookin' for witnesses, not suspects," he said belligerently as soon as he spotted Garrett.

"I've just come back to return this jackknife, which Mr. Lester says belongs to you." Garrett held out the knife he had found near the crime scene.

Bolt took it. "By God, this is mine. Where on earth did you – ?" He stopped in mid-sentence. His eyes blazed. "What's goin' on here?"

"I found it about thirty feet or so from one of the Chryslers last Saturday – where you must have dropped it."

"You're tryin' to set me up!"

"You were near the scene of that argument, weren't you?"

"You can't ask me that question. You're not the police in this town."

"No, I can't. But I can pass along this information to someone who can."

Bolt's jaw dropped. "I just wanted to avoid trouble," he said. "And Derbyshire was not interested in askin' anybody there on Saturday questions about what they might've seen."

"That's true, isn't it? Derbyshire is so sure he has his man, he isn't asking questions of anybody except Wilbur Bright."

"I didn't see nothin' that could help much."

"Just how much did you see?"

"I was pretty drunk. Matt was passed out. I tottered around looking for a place to take a leak. I headed for the big Chrysler, the Mayor's car. I thought it'd be fair if I pissed on his tires."

"And you saw Stanton and Bright?"

"Yeah. They were goin' at it hammer and tong. Bright kept yellin' somethin' about a ringer and Stanton was scoffin' at him, his dukes up. Then Stanton picks up a horseshoe and wallops the old guy. He falls back and Stanton comes at him again. But the old guy gives him a shove, to save himself – he had blood runnin' down his face. And Stanton falls sideways and hits his face on the runnin'-board of the sedan. I think to myself, 'Good for you, old man. The bugger got what he deserved.'"

Garrett was excited. Here was what he was after. If Bolt had seen Uncle Wilbur leaving the scene while Stanton was still on the ground with the horseshoe in his hand, then Uncle Wilbur was off the hook, for he had not been present when the fatal blow had been struck.

"Did you see Wilbur Bright stagger away, hurt?" he asked.

Bolt hesitated, then said, "No. I was drunk. I was happy that Stanton got decked. I went back to wake up Lester and tell him the good news."

"So Wilbur Bright was still between the two cars when you turned away?"

"That's right. I got back to Lester and kicked him awake. Then we heard the hue and cry."

This, if true, was disappointing. Uncle Wilbur was still present and could conceivably have finished off the fallen ringer before he himself staggered away. But it was more likely Bolt himself who had done the deed in his drunken stupor.

"You're sure you didn't go over there, pick up the horse-shoe and strike Stanton with it?"

"'Course I didn't! Hey, I thought you were lookin' for wit-nesses? And here you go accusin' me of murder. And you're just the village cop! Well, I'm gonna let Detective Derbyshire know what you've been up to!"

"Go ahead. And you'll be sure to tell him everything you've told me," Garrett said, turning to leave. "And explain why you haven't bothered to step forward."

Bolt paled. "You bastard!" he shouted at Garrett's back.

The phone was ringing when Garrett got back just before noon.

"Garrett?" It was Bull Derbyshire.

"Speaking."

"I've got the pathologist's report here. I've been ordered by my chief to pass it along to you," Bull said, the reluctance clear in his voice. "As a matter of courtesy," he added coldly.

"What did he find?"

"The blood on the horseshoe was both AB and RH negative. AB is the victim's blood type. RH negative, a rare type, is Wilbur Bright's."

"That merely suggests that Wilbur was hit by the horseshoe, probably before the fatal blow hit Stanton."

"Stanton's fingerprints were on the shoe, along with the blurred prints of three others."

"You were unable to match them with Captain Bright's?"

"That's right. But we've got him and his blood at the scene. And no sign of any third party."

"He may claim self-defence. After all he must have taken the first blow."

"Not a chance," Bull said with some glee. "The doc says that Stanton was lying prone on the ground when he took that fatal blow. As you suspected, he did hit his cheek on the running-board of the sedan – there were fragments of rubber in the contusion. So, it was a cowardly act upon an unconscious or dazed man. It was first degree murder."

"I see."

"And now that my official duty is out of the way, I've got something more important to discuss with you."

"What would that be?" Garrett was sure he knew what was coming.

"I got a call from Matt Lester a few minutes ago."

"Yes. I talked with him this morning.."

"You questioned him and Bolt this morning, that's what you did."

"I had a hunch they might be witnesses to help seal your case."

"I'll bet you did!" Bull's deep voice shook with anger. "What the hell do you think you're doin' playin' detective behind my back?"

"I never pretended I was officially investigating," Garrett said lamely.

"But you quizzed Lester and Bolt like they were suspects!"

"Did they happen to give you the substance of our interviews?"

"Why should they? You had no business conducting them. And I'm giving you fair warning. If I hear of one more misstep on your part, I'll have your badge and then your hide!" It was clear that Derbyshire was enjoying himself, getting revenge for being accused of cheating perhaps.

"Bolt was at the scene," Garrett said quietly in the sudden silence. "He saw a lot of what happened. Perhaps he knew more than he told me."

There was a long pause.

"He saw the confrontation?"

Garrett decided not to tell him how he had used the jackknife to get this admission out of Bolt. "He has quite a detailed story to tell you. You can quiz him when he comes in to make an official complaint," he said with relish.

"Does his story jibe with my case?" Derbyshire felt constrained to ask, though there was a hollow sound at the centre of the deep basso.

"It does, though he didn't actually see Captain Bright strike Stanton with the shoe."

"Damn! We don't want the bugger going for self-defence."

Garrett sighed. In for a penny, in for a pound. "There were threats exchanged," he said.

"Bolt heard them?"

"Ah, no. In fact it was Mayor Portland Gage."

A shuddering pause, then, "You questioned the Mayor?"

"Not really. I was there on other business, which you'll hear about soon, and he offered the information to me."

"If you've upset the Mayor, I'll have you skinned alive and mounted on the City Hall steeple!"

"He was most agreeable."

"What sort of threats did he hear? You might as well spit it all out."

"They threatened to harm one another," Garrett said softly.

"Aha! That's what we need. We've got Bright in a rage at the ceremony and then threatenin' the fellow – before doin' him in."

"You can thank me later."

"Perhaps you're not as bad as you appear to be," Derbyshire said generously. "But my warning still goes. Keep your nose clean. And if you do hear anything locally, you call me, straightaway."

"I'll be sure and do that."

Derbyshire hung up without saying goodbye.

Things looked even worse for Uncle Wilbur now. As Garret complained later in the afternoon to Maud Marsden in her dairy-bar, the more he investigated the more he made certain Uncle Wilbur would be convicted. Even a self-defence plea seemed highly dubious.

"I've got to find a way to break Bolt down," he was saying. "Or find myself another witness."

"You haven't asked Breezy to put the word out?"

"Not yet. But I guess I should do so right away, eh?"

"I'll do it for you," she grinned. "Breezy always enjoys taking advice from his favourite councillor."

"Thank you."

"But you're not going to be able to get at Bolt, are you? Derbyshire is a powerful man. He might not get your badge, but he can make life in these parts intolerable for you. And remember, he has jurisdiction over major crimes. You may have to work with him in the future."

"But what else can I do?"

Maud thought about this. "Well, let's assume it's not Bolt."

"All right, what then? Who's left?"

"Someone not yet in the picture."

"True, but how do we get near him – or her?"

"You need to find out more about Roy Stanton himself." She went to serve a young girl who had come in for a brick of Neapolitan ice cream. Then she returned and said, "If Bolt didn't do it, then Stanton must have had some other enemies."

"But he's only been in the City for three months. Hardly time to make a mortal enemy, is it?"

"Well, he must have made one. That blow was vicious, the product of hate, I'd wager."

"True. But where do I start?"

"With the only man we're certain knew something about him."

Garrett smiled. "Of course. The real Ray Stanton."

Garrett determined to go and see Ray Stanton first thing in the morning. He had to find out as much as he could about Roy Stanton's past, and particularly his three-month stay in Petroleum City. And if he did develop leads, he would have to pursue them without attracting Bull Derbyshire's attention. Meantime, he had his evening patrol to do, the highlight of which was his visit with Breezy outside his shop (he lived in an apartment over it). Breezy had not yet made his pilgrimage to the City to convey the Council's generous offer of a rematch, provided the City use Tug Mason and either Archie Bolt or Matt Lester, all three of them veterans of past encounters. He promised Garrett he would do so the next day. "We'll win that trophy proper this time," Breezy had exulted.

Garrett finished his rounds by seven-thirty. He had a cold supper and tried to settle into his mystery novel. But although his days were proving to be more involved than he had expected, the evenings were long and tedious. He no longer, he realized, wanted to live alone. He thought about getting a dog or a cat. He found himself wishing the phone would ring, that Prudence Shannon would call about her prowler, who had apparently stopped his marauding. It would give him an excuse to drop in on Susan Shaw, whom he was quite worried about. She had enough on her hands with young Davie, and now Uncle Wilbur had to be a major concern. Perhaps he would just go over there without an excuse.

But the phone did ring.

"Police house."

"Come quick. I've got a peeping Tom!"

It was not Prudence.

"Who is this?"

"Eunice Potter. The postmistress."

Eunice Potter lived on King Street, just around the corner from the police house. Garrett was there in less than a minute. Eunice met him at her front door.

"You'll have to excuse my kimono," she said, her blond curls bobbing. "I was just getting ready to tuck into bed with a good book."

"Where did you see the peeping Tom?"

"In my bedroom window," she said, stepping aside and waving him in.

Garrett stepped right into the living-room. It was neat and tidy, and very, very feminine. There were ruffled doilies on the arms of the chesterfield and two matching, mauve chairs. The lamps had frills and furbelows. The curtains were lacy and puffed out as if a breeze were blowing through them. The carpet was Persian and undulating with nymphs and cherubim in various states of interconnection.

"Right this way," she said, walking before him so that he could not be unaware of the body moving boldly beneath the pink chenille of the robe.

"You saw this fellow clearly?" Garrett said, following her at a safe distance into a hallway at the end of which stood an open door.

"He stared right in at me, bold as brass!"

Garrett and Eunice entered the bedroom. The bedspread – a garish, flower-splashed affair – was pulled back and the sheets turned down. Garrett could smell attar of roses as heavy as incense in the air.

"I had just finished putting on my nightgown, thank goodness" she said, alerting him as to what silky delights lay under the robe, "when I looked up and there he was!"

"In that window there?"

"I could see all of his face above the sill. He was either very tall or standing on his tiptoes."

"I see. Did you recognize him?"

"Gracious, no. It was some stranger. Some tramp off the boats, I expect."

Unlike Prudence, Eunice was not in the least alarmed, but rather more indignant and not a little excited either by the abrupt appearance of the peeping Tom or the arrival of the village constable.

"What did he look like?"

"Like the bogey man. He had big saucer eyes and a long nose and a high forehead with hair spilling over it. Crazy, I'd say. Belonged in the loony bin, he did. He give me such a fright."

Eunice did not look in the least frightened. She pulled her robe more closely about her throat, but it was not a gesture born out of fear.

"I'll check outside to see if he left any footprints."

"What good will that do?"

"Well, if we catch the fellow, we can match his shoe-prints and prove our case."

"Oh, how clever," Eunice said, batting her lashes. It was at this point that Garrett realized she had not removed her makeup. Her lashes were artificially lengthened, her cheeks faintly rouged, and her lips a deep blood-red.

"I'll just be a minute."

"And I'll put the coffee on."

Garrett sighed, but went about doing his duty. He went out the back door and walked around to the bedroom window. There was a large flowerbed just below it. Garrett shone his flashlight on it. There were no footprints. No-one had stood directly below this window, though it was conceivable that a tall man – over six feet – might have stood outside the flowerbed on the grass and leaned over to peer in – perhaps an experienced peeper who was very wary of leaving anything behind.

Was the village saturated with peepers and prowlers? It seemed so. Certainly the single ladies thought so. He went back in and reported what he had found.

"I thought he was a tall guy," Eunice said from the kitchen doorway, "because he had a long nose and a long face."

Garrett felt unable to comment.

"Just make yourself comfortable on the chesterfield, Constable. Or should I call you Stan?"

"Stan is fine, Miss Potter."

"Eunice, please. A woman of my age does not like to be referred to as 'Miss.'"

Garrett went and sat down on the chesterfield, sinking several inches into its soft depths. A minute later Eunice arrived with a tray of coffee and cookies. She set it down on the coffee-table and poured out two cups.

"Cream and sugar?"

"Just black, please."

She smiled with her blood-red lips. "I like a man who takes his coffee black. It's a sign he knows what he wants." She leaned over to pour a bit of cream into her own cup, revealing the upper curves of her breasts.

"You live all alone in this house,?" Garrett asked.

"I do. And I know the next question you're going to ask."

"You read minds?"

"I know men. You're wondering what a thirty-three-year-old woman who is not unhandome is doing unmarried and living alone?"

Garrett smiled. "Something like that crossed my mind."

"It's a long story. My mother left me this house and a size-able legacy five years ago, so I have the luxury of working merely to keep myself occupied."

"That explains the house."

"It does. As for the other, well, I had my great love when I was nineteen."

"Oh," Garrett said, suddenly wondering, to his surprise, what sort of beauty this handsome woman would have been at that tender age.

"His name was Bill. We were engaged."

Garrett did some rough calculations and said, "And Bill went off to war?"

Sadness filled her face, the way it had likely done every time the story got retold. "Yes. Overseas. To Belgium."

"Leaving you to wait for him?"

"Yes. He fought at St. Eloi and Vimy." She sipped at her coffee. "He survived until the very last week of the war. Then he got hit by a stray shell. There wasn't enough left of him to bury."

"I'm sorry."

"Why don't we spruce up this coffee," she said suddenly. "I've got some good whiskey in the cupboard over there."

Garrett was startled to hear himself say, "That would be nice."

She went to the cupboard, returned with the whiskey and poured a dollop into each coffee cup. "I hear you lost your wife," she said.

"Yes, Anna died two years ago, of an aneurysm."

"That's terrible. And you had been married – "

"Eight years. Eight wonderful years."

"I had only one. But it seemed enough."

They drank.

"I still keep a book of poems that Bill sent me for a Christmas present. A book of love poems."

"That was sweet of him."

"Here, I'll show it to you." She got up and went back to the cupboard for the book.

Garrett took the keepsake in his hands. He read the inscription. Eunice poured another dollop of whiskey into the remains of their coffee. The cookies remained untouched.

As Garrett browsed through the book, a postcard fell out. He picked up and read the name of the addressee on the front side: "Bunny." The card itself contained a Shakespearean sonnet. She watched him closely as he read it through.

"Lovely words, eh?"

"You were his 'Bunny'?" he said, touched.

She laughed. "Oh, no. 'Bunny' was some girl he saw before me. I always kept the card he never sent her after he met me – as a reminder of how we first met and of his faithfulness ever after."

"I kept a number of items to remind me of Anna."

"The hardest part, I think, is that one keeps living, keeps on with life."

"It doesn't seem right or fair, does it?"

"But we can't stop ourselves. And it hurts."

Eunice, who was now seated beside him, leaned against his shoulder. "But we can't live in the past forever, can we?"

They met halfway. Her lips were warm, inviting, forgiving.

Suddenly he broke away. He stared at the carpet. She took his chin in both hands.

"It's too soon for you, isn't it?"

He nodded.

"And you'll come again if that peeping Tom returns, won't you?"

There was no peeping Tom, but he heard himself say, "Yes. Any time."

# CHAPTER 9

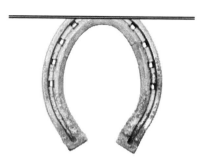

Although it was somewhat after the fact, Garrett decided to ride around the village one more time, just in case there really had been a prowler. He also wished to settle his nerves, as the near seduction (by one or both of them) had left him shaken. He realized that some day he would find another woman attractive – like Susan Shaw for instance – but he did not want things to happen like that episode back at Eunice Potter's. Each of them had been equally vulnerable and predatory. And perhaps each would have regretted their actions. Or, worse, have not regretted them when their daily existence was predicated upon faithfulness.

At any rate he found no trace of a prowler. The streets were empty except for the area between the docks and the Regency Arms. As he rode by Susan Shaw's, he noticed her lights still on. Without forethought he went up and knocked at the front door.

Susan answered, looking wan and tired. But she smiled as brightly as she could when she saw who it was.

"Come in, Stan. You look worse than I do."

"I just stopped by to see how you are getting on."

"Well, come in and have a cup of tea. It's already made."

Without any additives, he hoped.

"Yes, I will, thank you."

"I'll get the tea."

He sat down on one of the sofa-chairs, well away from the chesterfield. He wished to avoid any rematch with the bout of guilt and desire he had just experienced. Susan was also an attractive woman and, for better or worse, reminded him a great deal of his Anna. Not so much in her looks – Anna had light brown hair, blue eyes and freckles – but in her beauty and manner, in the sense of repose at the heart of her, despite the blows fate had dealt her.

Susan returned with the tea things, served a cup to Garrett, then perched on the edge of the chair opposite him. The room was comfortable, lived-in, with the feel of a country parlour about it – like the front room of his parents' house, the one he had grown up in.

"How is Uncle Wilbur doing?"

"Not good, I'm afraid. He doesn't like being cooped up at the best of times."

"When will his bail hearing be?"

"Tomorrow morning. I was told by Detective Derbyshire that the Crown will be asking for two thousand dollars."

"That much?"

"Yes, and I've got to find a way to raise it."

"You can't mortgage the house, you told me."

"I can't. But I've got jewels and silver, family heirlooms left to me by my mother. I can sell those. But they won't bring in two thousand."

"I'll go to Breezy in the morning and see if the town can help."

"Even if we get Uncle out, there'll be nothing left for a lawyer."

Garrett could see she wanted to cry but was holding back the tears for his sake.

"How is Davie managing?"

"All right, I think. He lives in his dream world out there in his fort," she said, obviously wishing such a world were possible for her.

"There's going to be a rematch with the City. Your uncle will like that."

"So he was right about Stanton after all?"

"He was. But I imagine that's of little solace to him at the moment."

Garrett's remark was interrupted by a clatter from upstairs.

"What was that?" he said, thinking "burglar."

"Just Davie coming in the upstairs window from the fort."

"Upstairs window?"

"He gets onto the flat part of the roof from the tree outside his window and goes in through the dormer."

"He doesn't sleep out there in the cold nights, does he?"

"No. We have a deal. Though he's past his deadline tonight."

Something important, something he had overlooked until now, occurred to Garrett. "Do you mind if I speak to the boy before he goes to sleep?"

"Oh, please do. His uncle always tucks him in."

Garrett made his way upstairs and found Davie sitting on his bed.

"The bike works great, Mr. Garrett," he said, giving Garrett a welcoming grin.

"Been visiting your fort, eh?"

"I feel safe out there. It's my favourite spot in all the world."

"Tell me, were you out there on Monday night a week ago?"

"I was out there every night last week."

"Do you see people coming and going in the lane?"

"Yes, but not many people use the lane."

"Please, think back to a week ago Monday night. Did you see anyone, anyone at all in the lane that runs behind your house?"

"After dark, you mean?"

"Yes. After dark."

Davie didn't hesitate. "No. Not Monday night. No-one came or went. "

"What about Tuesday night?"

"I did see someone that night. A man."

"Someone you know?"

"No. A stranger, though I couldn't see his face or anything."

"Where was he?"

"That's the funny part of it. He was sneaking through Miss Shannon's hedge into the Turnidge's back yard."

Garrett held his breath. "Go on."

"He sneaked along behind Turnidge's, then did something very strange."

"Strange?"

"Yeah. He tapped on the back window. The kitchen window, I think."

"Then what did he do?"

"I was thinking maybe he was a robber or something when he turned and went in the back door."

"Just walked in?"

"Well, he turned the door handle, real gently, and the door opened."

"Did you see him come out?"

"No. I thought he must be okay if he just walked in. I turned over and must have fallen asleep for a bit."

"You saw or heard nothing else?"

"No."

"Thank you for this, Davie. You've answered a question that's been nagging me for a week."

Garrett said goodnight and went back downstairs.

"You look worried," Susan said. "Is Davie all right?"

"He's fine, but he may have seen the prowler that's been upsetting Prudence Shannon."

"I know. She's been on about it, though it's been a few nights now since she's had the wits scared out of her."

"I've got to check something out. Thanks for the tea. And don't worry. We'll find some way to get that bail money."

"Thanks," she said, and there was more than thanks in her eyes.

Garrett hurried out. But he didn't go far. The Turnidge house sat between Susan's place and Prudence Shannon's.

There was the faint glow of a lamp in the front window. Garrett walked onto the verandah and knocked on the door.

After a long while the door opened a crack.

"Oh, it's you, Constable. What do you want?"

Wilma Turnidge was still dressed, but her hair was in disarray and her eyes red-rimmed from weeping. She looked distressed.

"I have some disturbing news about a burglar that you need to know about.," Garrett said.

"Oh." She looked startled and befuddled.

"May I just stop in for a moment?"

"Oh, yes. Come in. The place is a mess. I've had a bad bout of hay fever today and haven't done a stitch of housework."

The living-room looked slightly dishevelled but was a darn sight neater than Garrett's house. He stood in the open vestibule.

"I've had a report, ma'am, that a burglar was seen entering your house by the kitchen door a week ago Tuesday."

"Last week, you mean?" Something like fear was creeping into her face.

"Yes. A strange man tapped at your window and then went in the back door."

Wilma's eyes grew round with fright. "Oh, Constable, you won't tell my husband, will you? You see, I'm supposed to lock all the doors, but some of the time I forget, and he gets very cross with me."

"So you didn't hear the burglar come in?"

"Oh, no. I was upstairs. I'd gone to bed early to listen to Lux Radio Theatre. Orville doesn't get home till eleven-thirty or so from his afternoon shift. If I heard anything, I would have been too scared to scream. But I didn't."

"And you didn't find anything missing the next morning?" She thought about this. "No. Nothing was taken. But I should have locked that door, shouldn't I?"

"Perhaps the thief heard the radio and realized someone was at home. Burglars rarely harm anyone. And they prefer empty houses."

"And I had all the lights out, didn't I?"

Garrett remembered that fact. He had rapped on the door that Tuesday and got no answer. The burglar may still have been inside.

"Well, Mrs. Turnidge, I suggest you always lock your doors, even in a friendly village like Port Eddy. And I don't see any need to tell your husband."

"Oh, thank you, Constable. Thank you."

Something was not quite right here, but Garrett decided to press no further. He wished Wilma goodnight and left.

On Thursday morning, Breezy Harkness was escorted into Mayor Portland Gage's spacious office by his blond secretary. The horseshoe trophy gleamed conspicuously from its plant-stand. Breezy tried not to look that way, but Gage had placed it so strategically in the room that it was nigh impossible not to notice it. However, it would not be here much longer, Breezy thought, if there was justice in the world.

"I suppose you've come to gloat," Gage said.

"Not at all, Portie, not in the least. I trust, though, that you have checked out our claim and found the real Ray Stanton living on Maxville Street?"

"Sadly, we have. But I assure you, sir, we were as bamboozled as you were. And the crook goes and gets himself murdered to boot." The Mayor's dewlaps shook with indignation.

"So the question now is, what is to be done in the circumstances?"

"Technically, you can demand the match be declared forfeit and the trophy returned to you," Gage said. He looked longingly at the silver cup. He hadn't yet told Breezy but he had already had the names of the City's tossers inscribed there.

"Technically," Breezy mused, enjoying very much his delaying the message he knew he had eventually to deliver.

"But, Breezy, old chap, we are men of the world, aren't we? Is there not some way we can negotiate a more reasonable outcome?" Gage reached for the cigar box and drew out a lusty-looking Cuban stogie. "Cigar?"

"Don't mind if I do."

"Straight from Havana."

"I'll light it up later."

"Now what's this 'technically' business? Did I hear a hint of something less final in your voice?"

Breezy, who had worked this plan over and over in his mind, said with a resigned sigh, "Well, my council has advised me that they would like the match to be forfeit. The way they see it, and I don't necessarily agree, is that a ringer is a ringer and it is your responsibility to check the bona fides of your players."

"Would you care for some whiskey? I've got single malt."

Breezy waved off the offer.

"You said you yourself didn't necessarily agree?"

"That's right. I felt there was some small room for negotiation. Among men of the world."

"You have been given some leeway, then?"

"I have," Breezy said nicely.

"Perhaps we could stage a rematch. We'd use Bolt or Lester. They're not ringers, as you well know."

"I could recommend such a possibility to my council, especially, as you say, you were bamboozled by Stanton as much as we. He was diabolically clever, wouldn't you say?"

Breezy enjoyed watching the grimace on the Mayor's face as he had to swallow the obvious truth that he had been hoodwinked by a low-life like Roy Stanton.

"Too clever by half," Gage pointed out. "Somebody paid him back."

"The trouble is, I'd have to go out on a limb with my council" Breezy continued. "I'd have to stick my neck a long ways out."

The Mayor sat back on his high perch, feeling at last on more solid ground, the high ground even. "You are suggesting, I take it, that some compensation might be in order for one's sticking one's neck out?"

"The thought crossed my mind." Many times, Breezy mused.

"What sort of compensation were you thinking of?"

"I understand our Conservative MLA, Mr. Thompson, is retiring before the next election.

Gage looked alarmed. "Meaning the nomination would be open?"

"That had occurred to me, yes."

"But I have only limited influence on such matters. Perhaps you're overestimating my powers, good sir."

"Not in the least. All I want is a word put in on my behalf."

Gage, of course, was considering a run at the nomination himself, but he said with blithe confidence, "Consider it done."

"You understand that I have no way of guaranteeing I can sway my council," the Reeve intoned.

"You understand that I have no way of guaranteeing you a nomination?" the Mayor intoned.

"A rematch it is, then."

"A rematch it is."

On his Thursday morning patrol Garrett stopped at the barbershop and told Breezy about the need for bail money. Breezy suggested that a bingo be set up for Friday night, and that some sort of raffle be organized for the rematch, now scheduled for two o'clock Saturday. Breezy, who had just retuned from City Hall, had of course found his meeting with Mayor Gage more than satisfactory. He had even offered to let the trophy remain in the Mayor's office until it was won back on Saturday.

Garrett then took Maud Marsden's advice and rode down to the City to see Ray Stanton. But he could not get Stanton to come to his door, despite his pleas and protestations. Discouraged, he pedalled home and went to inform Susan of the money-raising plans. There he got a shock.

"I've just got off the phone with Derbyshire," Susan said at the door, looking distraught.

"And?"

"And Uncle Wilbur has confessed to the murder."

"But he's told us he didn't do it," was all Garrett could think to say.

"Of course he didn't do it. It's because I was foolish enough to tell him of my plans to sell my family heirlooms. He wants to save us all a lot of bother."

"That's absurd."

"I know. But he's a stubborn and loving old man."

"What can we do?"

Susan grimaced. "I hate to ask you this because I know what Detective Derbyshire has threatened you with, but would you mind going to see my uncle? I will, too, but I won't get to first base with him. Maybe you can talk some sense into him."

"The jail is in the basement of City Hall, isn't it?"

"I know, and I hate to ask but – "

"But I'll find a way to avoid Derbyshire. Don't worry."

"Thank you."

"Thank me only if I can get the old fellow to change his mind."

The city hall, police headquarters and jail were in the same complex of buildings in the city centre. One advantage that Garrett had in remaining inconspicuous was that the area at any given time sported several police officers coming and going. He could use his uniform as a form of camouflage. He rode his bike to the rear of the complex and locked it in the bike rack. He slipped into the back door that led down to the jail. The jailer sat at a desk in a small vestibule. He looked up at Garrett.

"You new on the job?" he said.

"Yes, but not on the City force. I'm the constable in Port Eddy."

"What can I do for ya, Constable?"

"I've been asked by Mrs. Shaw, Wilbur Bright's niece, to take a message to him."

"Why can't she do it herself?"

"She's, ah, indisposed at the moment."

The jailer frowned, paused, but said, "I can't see it doin' any harm. After all, you're one of us, ain't ya?"

"Thank you, sir."

Garrett was shown into a small cramped cell. Uncle Wilbur looked up wearily, not recognizing Garrett at first.

"I've come from Susan," Garrett said, sitting on the bunk beside Uncle Wilbur.

"Oh, it's you, Garrett? I figured she'd come but she's sent you instead, eh?"

"She'll be along this afternoon. She's shocked, as I am, that you've confessed to a crime you did not commit."

Uncle Wilbur looked grave as he said, "But I'm seventy years old. I've lived a long and happy life."

"But you didn't kill that man!"

"I may have."

"What do you mean?" Garrett said, startled.

"You see, when Stanton hit me with that horseshoe, I was dazed and woozy. I remember seeing red and feeling very, very angry. I thought he would hit me again, and I lashed out, and he fell back. I don't honestly remember anything else until I found myself standing in the marsh, bleeding from the scalp."

"So you think you could have killed a man and not remembered doing it?"

"It's quite possible, isn't it? Who else could have done it? There was only Stanton and me, the impostor and the man determined to expose him."

"But with a good lawyer you could plead self-defence or at least extreme provocation. He was after all a strapping thirty-five-year-old and you an elderly gentleman."

"You and I both know that I can't afford a fancy lawyer."

"So you're determined to stick with this foolish confession?"

"I've made Bull Derbyshire a happy man."

"But think of the shame and scandal you'll bring on Susan and little Davie."

The old man sighed. "I've thought about that. But a lot of damage is already done, isn't it? The whole county knows I've been arrested and charged. Besides, they're young. They'll get over it."

"Susan might, but Davie won't," Garrett said, hating himself as he did so.

"Well, what's done is done, lad."

Garrett admired the old captain's resolve to do what he thought was in the best interests of his family. It was always possible that, deep down, he believed he had done it. After all, there were no other candidates for the crime, and Garrett was acutely aware that he had failed to produce one. In fact he had made the case against Uncle Wilbur even more air-tight than it had been. It was now first-degree murder, for that fatal blow had been a cowardly strike upon a helpless victim.

"Well, please think about retracting your confession, sir. In the meantime, I intend to keep searching for the real murderer."

He didn't mention that he had only one slim lead to follow: interrogating Ray Stanton about his murdered brother. And even that wasn't going well.

Uncle Wilbur thanked Garrett for coming. Garrett left, feeling very much a failure.

Garrett went straight to Stanton's house on Maxville Street. But his steady knocking was met by silence. There was no doubt Stanton was home, but he refused to answer the door. Garrett rode home disconsolately. He stopped at Susan's to tell her about his abortive visit with Uncle Wilbur.

"He's a stubborn old man," Susan said, exonerating Garrett.

Garrett tried to cheer her up by talking about the bingo and the raffle.

"Breezy loves a challenge," Susan said, "as long as he's somewhere in the limelight. He'll canvass the village businesses for prizes for the raffle."

"Don't worry, we'll get your uncle out of jail, and we'll get him acquitted," Garrett said with as much conviction as he could muster.

It was Friday afternoon before Garrett could get back to Stanton. Friday morning was consumed by petty episodes that required his professional intervention. There was a spate of truancies (not including Davie). Garrett found himself pedalling all over the village in quest of boys playing hooky. One group he caught smoking behind the shed at the docks. Another was a lone grade-eighter, whom he found crying behind the pool hall. He took the lad home rather than have him face Brute Fagan, who had already strapped him once. He suggested his mother report the boy had taken ill at recess and not returned to the school. Then a group of sailors from a just-arrived ship caused a disturbance at the Regency Arms, and while it was quickly quelled with the appearance of the local constable, Hopalong Hitchins begged Garrett to keep a close watch on the place for the rest of the day.

But by late afternoon he was able to slip away at last. This time when Garrett arrived at Stanton's he had a plan. At the front door, where he could not be seen from inside the house, he rapped and called out, "Royal Mail. Special delivery for Mr. Roy Stanton."

Very slowly the door eased open.

"I really must speak to you, Ray," Garrett said, putting his foot in the door.

"Oh, very well," Stanton said, stepping back to let Garrett in. "I was getting tired of hearing you knock anyways."

He followed Stanton into the kitchen, where he was preparing his supper.

"I've come to talk to you about your brother."

"All right, if you must. But there isn't much to tell." Stanton looked pale and weary. He had been through a terrible week, with his brother being murdered, himself being exposed as part of his brother's fraud, and the funeral on Wednesday that he could not attend.

"You've made your peace with the Mayor and the horseshoe committee?"

"I have. The Mayor was understanding, especially when he realized I had done nothing specific to aid Roy."

"I'm glad to hear that."

"What do you want to know about my brother?"

"Well, to be frank, I don't believe Wilbur Bright killed him. I'm trying to find out if Roy had any enemies, people who disliked him enough to murder him."

Stanton was taken aback. He leaned forward in his chair. "I thought the police were sure."

"They are, I'm not."

"I see. I'd like to help you but there's so little to tell."

"Roy had been here three months?"

"About that."

"Did anyone from the Toronto area come to visit him?"

"No-one. We stayed here together and saw no-one but the delivery boy."

"Any telephone calls?"

"One or two. Roy was inquiring about the horseshoe play-downs. I assumed those calls were regarding that."

"Surely Roy went out."

"Oh, yes. But, you see, we didn't talk much. We were never close. As kids, although only a year apart, we were entirely opposite. I was shy and retiring. He was boisterous and outgoing. When I became ill, in my teens, I moved in here with my parents. Roy seemed embarrassed by my behaviour – he said I just needed a swift kick in the pants – and he left us for the big city and bright lights."

"Was he attracted to the ladies?"

Stanton smiled warily. "That he was. Right from the time he was in grade eight. He had many girl friends. I assume, as he never married, that he continued to live the gay bachelor life."

"What did he work at?"

"He did something in the music business. Sales, I think. But I got the impression that he moved from job to job a lot. Then, of course, the jobs dried up. And he came back here – for his inheritance." This last remark was said with some bitterness.

"And he never found a job here?"

"As a matter of fact he did. A few weeks ago he got a part-time position at Keeler's Music Store on Water Street. Just five or six hours a week."

"So you can't think of anyone who would want to murder him?"

"No."

And Garrett was forced to leave matters there. His talk with Ray Stanton, however, had produced one further lead: the music shop, though Garrett realized how slim a lead it was. It was looking more and more as if Archie Bolt was the culprit and Garrett had no way of proving it. But a lead was a lead.

The proprietor of the music shop was happy enough to talk to Garrett, mistaking him no doubt for a City policeman. There were only two customers in the place, and they were in the sound booths listening to records for free.

"I'm here to ask you a few questions about your employee, Ray Stanton, as he called himself." Garrett said.

"Oh, the tosser that got murdered, you mean?"

"That's the one. Did you ever see him with anyone? With friends or cronies who might have come here to see him?"

"I don't allow that. But he was a chatty sort of fella. He spent a lot of time with some of the customers. And sold a lot of records."

"But no-one who particularly stands out?"

"I'm afraid not."

"Did he ever take any phone calls?"

"Let me think. The second or third day he was here, he got a call."

"Did he say who it was from?"

"No, but I gathered from the tone of the conversation – I wasn't listening in, mind you – that it was some woman. I warned him then about taking personal calls here."

"A woman?"

"Yeah. He kept calling her 'Bunny.'"

Bunny. Garrett was both puzzled and excited. Stanton was involved in some way with a woman called Bunny. And that was a name he had already heard, in Port Eddy at Eunice Potter's place. Eunice had said it was a pet name for an old flame of her dead fiancé. But was she telling the truth? Could she herself be Bunny? If so, then Roy Stanton had a connection of some sort with the village. Could Eunice have been a lover or girl friend of Stanton's a long while ago, before he left for Toronto? Had he tried to revive the relationship? Had something gone wrong? But what? Surely there had not been enough time for hatred to flare. But could it be husbanded for twenty years? Still, it didn't seem likely that the fatal blow had been delivered by a woman. But it was possible. Stanton lay dazed for several minutes, during which time anyone happening along could have picked up that horseshoe and done him in.

How should he proceed? He couldn't just go to Eunice Potter and accuse her of lying about being Bunny. What grounds did he have? Perhaps this Bunny was a girl from Eunice's past, one she did not remember. Where did that leave him? Looking in a village of six hundred and fifty people for someone who used to be called Bunny by her boy friend.

These thoughts were interrupted by Mr. Keeler, who hailed him from the doorway.

"Oh, by the way, I found these in the drawer used by Stanton to stash his belongings." He held out a fistful of papers.

Garrett took them. They were betting slips.

# CHAPTER 10

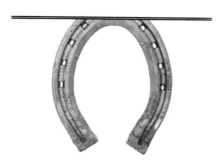

Garrett examined the chits. They were betting slips, all right. - for the horseshoe match between Port Eddy and Petroleum City. Most of the bets were for one or two dollars – on the City team. But two of them stood out from the others. A twenty-dollar bet with the name of Harvey Malcolm on it and a twenty-five-dollar bet in the name of Pat Evers. Could this be a motive for murder? Or a bit of payback that got out of hand? Had one of these men, having bet on the winning team against the bookmaker, accosted Stanton after the match and found him penniless or reneging on their deal? Perhaps Stanton had not been as dazed as had been thought. Perhaps he had had a brief argument with one of these punters, turned away and got bashed to the ground and then finished off? Anything was possible in the minute or two between Uncle Wilbur staggering off and Tug

Mason's arrival on the scene. Perhaps it was more like five minutes, as Uncle Wilbur could have stumbled and himself been near-comatose on the ground before getting up again and tottering away. What was more certain was that Stanton had had supreme confidence that he would win the match for the City and not only collect his hundred dollars from the Mayor, but had obviously planned to skip town with the punters' money – leaving them high and dry. Very likely he had had no intention of returning for that ceremony, trusting that the hundred dollars would be sent to his brother's residence. And if he were to lose the match, he could skip town anyway, with a smaller but still substantial stake. (The punters, alas, would have been assuming Ray Stanton was a lifelong resident of the City.)

What to do about all this? "May I borrow your phone book?" Garrett said to Keeler.

"Certainly," Keeler said, puzzled but pleased to cooperate with the law.

Garrett found addresses for Harvey Malcolm and Pat Evers. He located Malcolm's cottage on Vidal Street without any trouble. As he was approaching it he saw a curtain in the front window pulled open and whipped shut. Instinctively he headed around the corner and made for the back of the house. A picket fence blocked his path. He heard the rear door opening hastily. He vaulted the fence and landed hard. By the time he emerged into the back yard, all he could see was a lumpy figure struggling to get over a higher fence at the extreme rear portion of the property.

"Stop, Mr. Malcolm! I just want to talk to you!"

But talk, it appeared, was precisely what Malcolm did not want, at least not with anyone in uniform. The fellow tumbled onto the grass of a lane that ran behind the house. Garrett sprinted towards him as the man picked himself up and trundled down the lane. Garrett had to hop on top of the high fence, get his balance, and then jump down, giving the less-than-sleek fugitive time to put twenty yards between him and his pursuer. Garrett stood up running. He could hear the desperate panting of the fleeing man as he closed the gap between them. Just before they reached the side street, the race was over.

Harvey Malcolm lay gasping like a spent mullet on the grass of the lane. He needed air more than he needed to escape. Garrett could see that Malcolm was not accustomed to running or much physical movement of any kind. He was heavily fleshed with a round, red face, beady eyes buried in deep, sagging pouches, and a paunch that sat on his frame like a lumpy sack of flour. He was still wheezing when Garrett came up beside him.

"I had nothin' to do with it!" he cried between pants.

"I'm not here to arrest you, sir. I'm not even the City police. I'm Constable Garrett from Port Eddy."

The beady eyes widened a little. "Port Eddy?"

"Yes. Port Eddy."

"Then what do you want with me? I only set foot there for the holiday races and the horseshoe match."

"It's the horseshoe match I wish to ask you a question about."

Malcolm's expression darkened, deepening the crimson of his cheeks. "I got nothin' to say about that god-damned horseshoe match."

"You bet on it and lost your stake," Garrett said, helping Malcolm to his feet.

"How did you know that?"

"Let's go back to your house and we'll talk about it."

"I can't have folks seein' a cop come into my place."

"Okay, we'll talk here, shall we?"

"What's your interest in my bad bet?"

"Roy Stanton was murdered, remember."

"I read it in the papers."

"Were you at the horseshoe match?"

"Sure I was. You seem to know I had twenty bucks ridin' on the City team."

"How did you make the bet?"

"I went into the music store and Stanton was workin' in there. We got talkin', and he goes on about a new guy – a real ringer – who's gonna pitch shoes for the City this time and how he'd found a group of Port Eddy punters who were willin' to give odds on their team. I thought, this is like havin' the inside dope on a stakes race. Stanton was offering to hold the bets – to play bookie – and of course bet himself."

"I've seen the betting slips he kept. There were no punters from Port Eddy. You were being scammed."

"But he showed me his name in the phone book, and Keeler vouched for him. He was a slick talker, but I thought him a fool, a mark just waitin' to have his feathers plucked."

"And he suggested you spread the word that he was taking sure-fire bets?"

"He did, and I was happy to oblige."

"You know a lot of punters?"

"A few. Word gets around."

"So you must have been relieved when the City won."

"I was ecstatic. I'd won forty dollars. And my friends had cashed in as well."

"But when you ran into him after the match, you discovered he'd spent or stashed the money in his own sock?"

"But I didn't get to see him, did I? Somebody beat me to him."

"You didn't follow him when you saw him leave the presentation platform?"

Malcolm hesitated, wheezed once and said, "What if I did?"

"Well, you may have discovered him dazed from a previous altercation with an unhappy spectator, and when you demanded your winnings, you discovered he was planning to run off with your money, and so you decided to beat it out of him."

Malcolm paled, despite his flushed state. "I lost him in the crowd. But I knew where he lived, didn't I? And I had no reason to kill the guy. You can't get money out of a corpse."

"Did you go around to his place?"

"I did. And found out his brother lived there.. The guy was a phoney and a scam artist through and through."

"His brother wasn't holding the money?"

"No. He swore not. We were scammed good."

Garrett believed him. Where Roy Stanton had stashed the money might never be discovered. "You were. We all were. Stanton was an illegal ringer all along. The match has been declared void, so you would have lost your money any way."

"That bastard. He deserved to die."

"So you're denying you had anything to do with the man's death?"

"I live for money, Constable. Not revenge."

And, sadly, looking at him, Garrett was inclined to agree.

As he was about to leave, he said to Malcolm, "By the way, your secret's safe with me."

"What secret?"

"You're in the game yourself, aren't you?"

Malcolm reddened again, but said nothing.

Garrett laughed to himself: the bookie had been undone by a sharper bookie.

Pat Evers lived on Divine Street in the north-eastern part of the City near the outskirts. The house was unprepossessing to say the least. It was a clapboard cottage that had not seen paint since the Boer War. A rose-arbour that had once borne roses was overrun by rogue vines and leaned precariously to one side, like a drunken sailor. Vestiges of blue paint could be seen on the front door as Garrett raised the knocker and found it in his hand. He placed it on the stoop and rapped with his knuckles. There was no answer but he was certain he could hear someone moving around inside. He rapped again.

Something heavy and lumpish thumped against the inside of the door. He heard a breathy curse-word, then the knob turning slowly. The door at last opened on a large, blowsy female with bright, darting eyes and her hair swept upward in a bouffant wild enough to have nested several species of bird. She blinked, and Garrett caught the full force of her gin-laden breath and noted the extra-brilliant glaze of her stare.

"Yeah?" she said in a low, rumbling voice, the rumbling emanating from a deep-bosomed chest reminiscent of an ageing diva.

"I'm Constable Garrett of the Port Eddy police. I'd like to talk to your husband."

"Then you'll have to shout extra loud," she said with only a slight slurring, "'cause he's been dead for five years."

"I'm referring to Pat Evers. Have I got the wrong house?"

"Not if you're looking for Pat."

"Is he in?"

"You're lookin' at him."

Garrett felt himself blushing. "May I come in, ma'am? I've one or two questions I'd like you to answer."

"Why not? I've never been able to resist a man in uniform." She blinked hazily. "What did you say you were again? A colonel?"

"Just constable, ma'am."

"Well, Con-shta-ble, do come in. I do like a question or two from a man, so long as I can say 'yes.'"

She turned and waddled away from him. He could see now that the flowered print she had wrapped around her was really a dressing-gown that had been bleached once too often, its decorous blooms suffering the same fate as the roses on the arbour outside.

"Pardon the mess, constable, but my cleaning lady up and quit on me, " she said and added with a gusty bray, "last year."

The living-room was a dump. Magazines and old newspapers littered the couch and single chair, and on each end-table several overburdened ashtrays vied for space. On the coffee-table sat several glasses and two bottles of spirits, each of them half empty.

"I was just havin' a little pick-me-up," she said, waving him to the chair. "What's your poison? Gin or gin?"

"It's too early in the day for me," Garrett said, brushing away a tattered newspaper or two and sitting on the edge of the chair.

"It's never too early," she said, and batted her lashes at him. The cleft of her dressing-gown yawned open.

"You go ahead. Please."

"Thank you. You're a real gentleman, and we don't get many of them in this town." She poured herself a half-glass of pure gin with a trembling hand, took a swig, licked her large, mobile lips and said, "What gentlemanly questions do you have for me, good sir?"

"Were you at the horseshoe match between the City and Port Eddy?"

She blinked, stared at her gin as if she were giving the question her utmost consideration, and said, "You mean the one this year?"

"I do."

"Then, yes, I was. I was in the stands cheering on our lads." She rolled her eyes. "Tug Mason and I used to be an item, you know."

"No, I don't."

"Well, we were. But the bugger was more interested in tossin' horseshoes than he was in tossin' me, so I dumped him."

"I see. But you never lost interest in the game?"

She grinned conspiratorially. "Tug wasn't the only tosser in town, if you get my meanin'."

"Did you know the new man, Roy Stanton, or Ray as he claimed to be?" The chances of Pat Evers being Bunny were slim, but he couldn't afford to overlook any possible clue.

"I never met the little weasel." She patted the couch beside her. "Why don't you come over and sit beside me? I can answer your questions better if I can see you better."

"I'm quite comfortable where I am, ma'am."

"Jesus, no-one's called me 'ma'am' since I was school-teachin' a hundred years ago."

"You knew about Stanton through Harvey Malcolm?"

Pat Evers snorted. "That asshole."

"He came to you with a sure-fire scheme to make a little money?"

She smiled grandly. "A girl's gotta make money now, don't she? Especially when there's a shortage of suitable men to help with rent and groceries."

"Malcolm told you a legitimate ringer was going to join the City team and make them victorious for the first time in five years?"

"You been talkin' to the little shit."

"I have spoken with Mr. Malcolm."

"Well, he said the Port Eddy punters were so sure of a win they were givin' four-to-one odds. And he guaranteed we were gonna win. I laid out twenty-five bucks."

"And Malcom was right, eh? The City did win the match."

"And that Stanton fella goes and gets himself murdered, don't he? Takin' my money with him."

"You didn't try to recover it?"

"Since when was makin' book legal?" she said with a huge sigh, and poured herself another gin. "And the crook was dead, wasn't he?"

"You didn't see Stanton after the match?"

"I saw him around that platform."

"You didn't see him leave? You weren't tempted to follow him?"

"I saw him head into the crowd. I thought, 'I hope the little turd ain't about to take off with our money.' But then I thought he had to come back for the trophy and the photographer. I'd get to him then. Or I'd get to Harvey Malcolm."

"So you weren't worried?"

She laughed, somewhere between a snort and a guffaw. "Stupid me, I wasn't. But if I'd've known the low-life was runnin' off to get his head bashed in, I'd've trailed after him and wrapped a horseshoe around his neck!"

Despite her obvious motive, Garrett felt that Pat Evers would have been either too drunk or too hungover to have followed Stanton through that crowd to the parked sedans and done the deed. He had come up against another brick wall.

Pat Evers leaned forward to reveal four-fifths of her mammoth breasts. She flashed Garrett a lurid smile and said, "Now it's time for you to do what any honourable gentleman should do when there's a willin' lady in the room."

Garrett sprinted for the front door.

As he rode home, much discouraged, Garrett realized that he was down to a single lead in the case: the mysterious "Bunny."

# CHAPTER 11

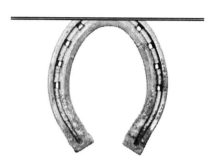

Garrett stopped in for a ginger-ale float at the end of his late-afternoon patrol. At four-fifteen he had seen Sideways Slim and Davie Shaw racing along the river flats, their hair flying, their legs pistoning, and going so fast that, from his perspective on Huron Street, they looked like a pair of Piper Cubs preparing for flight.

Garrett asked Maud about Bunny.

"Bunny?" she said, mouthing the word. "Sounds like the kind of pet name that lovers use."

"That's probably the case." He did not tell her about Eunice Potter, hoping that Maud's memory might toss up that name and its association spontaneously. Besides, he did not wish to relate the details of his evening visit to Eunice's.

"I can tell you, I've been living in this village all my life, forty some years, and although we have a lot of nicknames, we've never had anyone, male or female, called Bunny."

"Would there be anyone else who might know?" Garrett felt himself clutching at straws.

"Well, there might be now. Just a minute." She went to wait on a sailor who had just come in and sat down at the far end of the counter. When she returned she said, "Miss Hannah would be the one. As librarian for over twenty years, she sees people's names on their library cards every day, and has a memory like an elephant."

"I'll try her, then. I'm desperate. I feel helpless – at a dead end."

"I hope you're not overlooking Matt Lester," she said.

"But Lester was comatose with drink at the moment of the murder."

"That's what he said, remember. And Bolt, as you told it to me, wandered off in time to see the initial argument and fight. Lester could have been trailing him. Bolt by his own admission was drunk and drifted away, he said, before the fatal blow was struck. It could have been Lester who slipped in and finished off poor Stanton."

"But Bolt says he returned to their hidey-hole behind the barn."

"Perhaps they're covering for each other. They are mates, after all."

"I hadn't thought of that. Perhaps they both contrived to kill their rival, or maim him. They both could be lying. And Bolt only admitted he had seen anything after I found his jackknife nearby. Those two are making it up as they go along."

"You'll need to talk to them again."

"How can I do that without alerting Derbyshire? Even now he may have heard that I visited Wilbur Bright in his cell."

"They'll both be at the match tomorrow, one of them competing no doubt. You'll have to think of some way of approaching them."

"I might try suggesting to one that the other had changed his story."

"Do it subtly, eh?"

"Subtle is my middle name."

Garrett walked across the street to the library. It was open on Friday afternoons. It was deserted now except for Miss Hannah at her desk. She looked up shyly.

"Constable Garrett, would you like to take out a book?"

"I will eventually raid your mystery section, Miss Hannah, but I've come today to ask you a strange question."

He told her about Bunny possibly being a girl from the Port he was trying to track down. If Miss Hannah was curious about his motive, she was too reticent to ask.

She gave his request some thought. "Well now, I do vaguely recall that name on one of my cards, but it must have been ages ago."

"Could you try and search your memory. It's important."

"I can do better than that. I never throw away any of my cards. I've got them all in back. What dates are we talking about?"

Garrett recalled what Eunice had told him. "Try looking in 1917 or 1918."

"It could take some time."

"That's all right. If you find who 'Bunny' belongs to, will you phone me at home?"

Miss Hannah blushed at the thought and cast her eyes down. "Yes, I'll do that, Constable."

Garrett thanked her and left. Once again there was tantalizing hope, however slim.

The bingo to raise money for Captain Bright's bail, which was set at two thousand dollars, was held on Friday evening in the Oddfellows Hall. The place was jammed, many of the crowd having made the trip from Petroleum City. Breezy Harker called the numbers, and the jackpot of twenty-five dollars was won by Miss Hannah Bristol, much to the chagrin of Hopalong Hitchins who had only one spot on his card left to fill. Over three hundred dollars was raised. Susan had taken her jewels and silver to be evaluated, but the money offered for them seemed ridiculously low, so Susan held off selling them. Even with the best price, the full amount of the bail money could not be raised quickly – if at all. But Susan was nonetheless buoyed by the spirit of her village and its efforts to help her. For the rematch, a number of raffle prizes had been donated and raffle tickets duplicated at the Edward Street school.

Except for the absence of Wilbur Bright and Roy Stanton, the rematch was pretty much a replay of the original. The crowd was numerous and boisterous. Tug Mason was back, flanked this time by Matt Lester, who had won a coin toss with Archie Bolt. Garrett was disappointed that it was Bolt who was not tossing because he had hoped to broach Lester in between games. However, as a contestant, Lester would be surrounded by well-wishers and committee members at all times.

The first game this week was a singles match between Tug Mason and Clem Murphy. Tug's first shoe was a resounding ringer, which brought the better-dressed section of the crowd to its feet. Then Clem Murphy stepped up and threw his first shoe. It dug in nicely but the tines appeared to be just short of the post. Bull Derbyshire trundled over and gave it a preliminary look.

"Too close to call," he announced.

Tug's second shoe thudded into it, however, which had the effect of driving Clem's shoe into scoring position while bringing Tug's up short. Perhaps the gods were with the underdog after all. Now all Clem had to do was toss a ringer for three points on the very first end. The crowd held its collective breath as Clem's toss turned elegantly one-and-a-half- rotations and clanged around the post. Three points for Port Eddy! Bull came over for a second look, but it was a formality only.

From the other end both players missed with their opening shots and scored ringers with their second. Garrett came over to see which of the errant shoes was closest to the post. Using one of the ringers he was able to get his first crude measurement, and was pleased to see that Clem's winning shoe was a good inch closer. He felt Derbyshire's breath on his neck and the wheeze of disappointment as the big detective conceded the point. It was four to nothing for Port Eddy.

Then both players got hot. On the next two ends they matched ringers, cancelling each other's score. Then Clem, now shooting first, missed his opening shot, and the crowd groaned in sympathy as the shoe spun around the post and whirled away out of scoring range. Tug promptly threw a ringer. Clem's next shot looked as if it might cover that one but it sat up in the dirt and leaned precariously against the post – acting as a barrier to Tug's next attempt at a ringer. Tug gave his shoe a couple of extra turns and it thudded into the leaner, spinning them both out of scoring range. Tug's ringer counted, making the score four to three.

In each of the next four turns, each player scored a three-point ringer by throwing two perfect ringers to his opponent's one, bringing the score to ten to nine. Business at the concession stands dried up as no-one wished to leave his place in the stands to buy a hot dog or a coke. Even the cheers faded as the close score and the tension brought each side to a near-silent and apprehensive watching. Tense oohs and aahs were the only sounds audible.

When the score reached twenty to nineteen for Tug Mason, the tension became unbearable. Children clenched their fists in their parents' palms. Lovers gripped each other by the fingers. Husbands and wives clutched for the first time in months.

Clem Murphy, his slim postmaster's hands trembling, raised his shoe to his lips, bussed it for good luck, and threw. The shoe could be heard whirling through the stilled air and the sound of its striking was as loud as a church bell on Armistice Day. The shoe spun and stuck. Tug Mason took a deep breath and matched Clem's ringer. This brought a stunted, hopeful cheer from the Petroleum City folks. Clem's next shot grazed the top of the post and buried, tine-first, into the dirt. It looked to be within scoring range. Now all eyes turned to Tug, who, this time, took two deep breaths and – did his eyes close? – tossed the shoe. It struck the post sideways and spun away. Garrett sighed as he realized he would have to make the crucial measurement. His rough measurement with a horseshoe was too close to call. Derbyshire, as his side, agreed. Garrett took out his tape. It was not difficult to measure Tug's shoe as it was flat in the dirt. It was three and one-sixteenth inches away. But Clem's shoe was on an angle, with the rounded part towards the post.

"You gotta keep your tape level with the post and the shoe," Derbyshire instructed him.

That was not easy to do. On his first try he got a reading of three and one-eighth inches, and he heard Derbyshire's grunt of satisfaction behind him.

"That was a bit on the tilt," Garrett said. "I'll try again, level, as you suggested."

"You get one more shot," Derbyshire said, "and that's it."

The crowd was beside itself. So much rested on this silly game, all out of proportion to its results. But the depression had battered Port Eddy particularly hard. Most of the layoffs at the refinery and rubber plant in the City had been Port Eddyans, though it might have just seemed so as a consequence of the paranoia that came with being a small village surrounded by a noisy, boastful metropolis. Clear victories were few and far between. Well, if they couldn't have jobs, then by God they might have the satisfaction of retaining the Horseshoe Trophy and bragging rights at the London regionals.

Garrett took the second measurement, then stood up slowly. "Point to the City, and the game."

He felt the full weight of the villagers' disappointment. But they still had two matches to go, though of course they would now have to win both of them. But their best player had just lost by two points. Matters didn't look promising. Breezy Harker stared at the trophy, sitting on its stand near the pits, and grimaced. The thought of it returning for a full year to Portland Gage's office was too galling to be borne.

The next match began: Matt Lester against Harold Cooper. It seesawed back and forth, as did the hearts and hopes of their respective supporters. Fortunately, from Garrett's point of view as an official, there were no close measurements, so that he and Derbyshire were rarely at close quarters. Derbyshire looked placid enough that Garrett was reasonably sure he hadn't learned of his visit to Captain Bright. The confession, alas, still stood like an albatross around Garrett's neck. More happily, Cooper won the match on his last toss, a ringer.

There was more relief than optimism in the village half of the grandstand. The doubles match would decide the issue. Again there was little to choose between the two teams. Stripped of their ringer, the City squad had its hands full. With the score tied at nineteen-all, both Cooper and Mason missed their shots. With one shoe each left, Mason threw a shoe that spun away from the post but was close enough to count. If Cooper couldn't match it, the City team could take the lead, one point away from victory. Cooper took a deep breath, strode forward and threw. His shoe hit short of the post, open-ended, and pitched forward. It struck the post and was still. Was it a leaner, for two points and the win, or was it merely closest to the post, for one point? Derbyshire bulled his way forward to make the determination. Garrett was immediately beside him.

There was dirt around Cooper's shoe. It would have to be brushed away carefully to reveal whether the shoe was leaning or just close to the post. Derbyshire used his fingers like a whisk, flicking off the dirt and exposing the shoe. Garrett watched for the slightest sign that Derbyshire was attempting to nudge the shoe down and away from the post. Derbyshire looked up at Garrett and gave him an ambiguous grin. Then he finished the job. There was a good inch of post showing below Cooper's shoe. It was leaning: for two points and the victory. Port Eddy had retained the trophy!

Garrett now looked for his chance to talk privately with Lester. But it was not to be. Lester stood on the platform while the trophy was being presented to a beaming Reeve. Then immediately after, while the City Reporter was taking triumphal photographs, Lester left with the Mayor's party and was whisked away in the big Chrysler.

Everything was going well, it seemed, except the murder investigation.

At six o'clock the phone call came.

"I missed the match searching my records," Miss Hannah said proudly. "But I found two library cards with the name Bunny on them. From 1918."

"Tell me, who was Bunny?" Garrett asked.

Hannah told him.

"Thank you," he said. "You've been a terrific help."

And he meant it, for he now knew who had killed Ray Stanton, and why.

He knocked on the Turnidge's back door, and it was answered by Wilma.

"Is your husband home?"

"No. But he's not at work. He works every other Saturday. He's just gone to the grocery store. He'll be back soon."

"I need to speak to you both, officially."

"Then you'd better come in."

Once again her eyes were red-rimmed, and she appeared positively haggard. He followed her into a living-room that looked as if it had suffered serious neglect.

"Pardon the mess. I haven't been feeling well lately."

"No need to apologize."

They sat down.

"Mrs. Turnidge, that burglar we talked about the other day. I now have reason to believe it was not a burglar."

She looked almost too weary to be alarmed. "What can you mean?"

"I think you know what I mean. The man was seen tapping at your window, as if he were giving some sort of signal."

"That's absurd," she said without much conviction.

"Then he went to the back door and let himself in."

"But I was upstairs and the door was unlocked, remember?"

"Yes. Waiting for your lover, Roy Stanton."

She hung her head. She began weeping softly. "Yes, it was Roy. Orville was at work."

"And Stanton had to sneak about like a thief because he wanted to make sure no-one saw him."

She looked up. "Yes, but it didn't work. That busybody across the street saw him leaving and told Orville."

"That's what I assumed happened. Your husband found out you were cheating on him."

"He's insanely jealous. He's practically kept me a prisoner here ever since." She began sobbing quietly. "I can't even go to the grocery store."

"I know of his jealousy, ma'am. I had to break up a disturbance last week in the Regency Arms, where he threatened a man he thought had made eyes at you."

"You have no idea what it's been like living with that man. We go nowhere. He keeps me cooped up like a tame rabbit. Then Roy came back."

"You and Roy had had a relationship many years ago?"

"Yes. During the war. We were just kids." She tried to smile. "But it was a passionate affair. We were very much in love. At least I was."

"And Stanton nicknamed you 'Bunny'?"

She was startled. "How could you know that?"

"It's a long story."

"Yes, he called me that. I was so proud of it that, for a little while, I signed my name Bunny Wilson."

"Then Stanton left town?"

Wilma looked devastated, as if she were reliving that long-ago betrayal. "He said he needed his freedom. He swore he would send for me when the time was ripe. He never did. I found out later there had been other girls, even when he was dating me."

"Like Eunice Potter?"

"Yes, before she got engaged."

And Stanton must have called her his 'Bunny' as well, Garret thought. He must have been quite the ladies man.

"But how could you know about Eunice?" Wilma said.

"People in the village have long memories," he said vaguely.

Wilma gave a little sob and said, "And just when I was having a little bit of happiness with Roy, he ups and gets himself killed."

"You knew about his scheme to pose as his brother?"

"Oh, yes. Roy was just like his old self, mischievous and full of schemes to get rich. But he'd fallen on hard times, like the rest of us, and was desperate for money. He learned that the mayor of the City was offering a hundred dollars under the table for anyone who could help bring the horseshoe trophy back to the City. Roy had been a champion tosser in Etobicoke. He practised for hours at a pit in his back yard. He was certain he could be a champion again."

"But he wasn't eligible under the rules?"

"No. So he browbeat his brother, who's a recluse, into letting him take his name. He altered his own birth certificate. It was great fun, watching him pull all of this off and being in on the secret." She sighed. "He loved me enough to let me keep it."

At this point the back door opened and a moment later Orville Turnidge came into the living-room. He started to say something sharp to Wilma when he spotted the uniform. He paled.

"Come right in, Mr. Turnidge. I need to speak with you."

"If it's about the burglar, I know all about it. I've ordered Wilma to lock all the doors and windows."

"There's no use pretending any longer, sir. I know who the visitor was."

Turnidge glared at his wife.

"I found out on my own," Garrett said. "And it's Roy Stanton I've come to discuss."

"What about him? He was a low-life who sneaked about seducing other men's wives. I can't say I'm sorry he's dead, can I?"

"But it was you, sir, who murdered him."

Turnidge gulped for breath. This was not something he expected to hear. "But the old captain did him in. The police say so."

"They will not believe that for long, for it is you, sir, who have the stronger motive, one of the strongest of all motives for a man easily jealous and not afraid to use violence to intimidate rivals. As you showed me last week at the Regency Arms."

Turnidge slumped back into a chair.

"I submit that when you discovered your wife's infidelity, you were enraged. Here was a man who dallied with women and seduced your wife in your own home. You must have contemplated killing him a dozen different ways."

"I didn't plan to kill him," Turnidge said, looking at his wife. "Honest, love."

"But you did," Garrett said.

"Oh, Orville, tell me you didn't."

"I just lost it when I saw him lying there." He looked back at Garrett. "Mrs. Jones across the street saw the fellow leaving here. She knew the Stantons as boys. She told me it was either Ray or Roy, but when I confronted my wife, she said it was Ray, the tosser."

Covering for her lover even then, Garrett thought.

"It's all my fault," Wilma sobbed. "Oh, God, but I'm so sorry."

"You were at the match," Garrett said to Turnidge, "and at the end of it you spotted Stanton heading for the men's, and decided to follow him. But you got caught up in the crowd, didn't you?"

"Yes. I wasn't sure where he was going. I just wanted to put my fist in his face. To take him down a peg or two. Wilma'd already phoned and told him to stay away, pretending I only suspected."

"But eventually you saw him and Captain Bright arguing over by the big cars?"

"Yes, they were going at it hammer and tong. Then I see Stanton hit the old fella with a horseshoe. When he tried for a second blow, the old fella pushed him off. He twisted and fell down. I saw the captain stagger off, bleeding. I went up to Stanton, who was on the ground moaning. He had hit his head on something. He was dazed. I-I saw red. There was a horseshoe lying on the ground. I picked it up and – " At this point he put his head in his hands and stopped talking.

"So you would have let an innocent old man hang for your crime?"

Turnidge looked up. "Oh, no. This thing's been tearin' me apart. I figured the old fellow'd get off on self-defence. Even so, I don't think I could've kept this to myself much longer."

"I've got to call the City police. I want you to stay right here until they come. I'll leave you and your wife alone for a few minutes."

Bull Derbyshire and two uniformed police officers arrived ten minutes later.

"I've got the killer of Roy Stanton in the living-room," Garrett said to him in the kitchen. "Orville Turnidge has confessed."

"Jesus Murphy, Garrett. What am I to do with two confessions?"

"Wilbur Bright confessed because he was confused and couldn't quite remember what did happen. And Orville Turnidge has just told me that he saw Captain Bright, whom he knows well, stagger away from a semi-conscious Stanton."

"So he went up and finished the job?"

"That's right."

"You people in the Port certainly take your horseshoes seriously."

"Stanton's being a ringer wasn't the motive. It was more ordinary than that: jealousy. Stanton was seeing Turnidge's wife on the sly. Turnidge found out."

"But how in blazes did an ordinary copper like you find this out? Did Turnidge come to you and confess?"

"He confessed only after it was clear that I had discovered his motive and explained to him how the murder actually took place."

Derbyshire glared at him. "There must've been a lot of luck involved," he said. "You ain't no detective."

"Of course not," Garrett said. "I'm only a village flatfoot."

Uncle Wilbur came home late that afternoon. Garrett was invited for a celebratory supper with the family. While they were eating desert, Breezy Harker appeared at the door.

"I thought I'd find you here," he said, beaming. "I been asked by the council to offer you our congratulations. The councillors, and me also, are mightily impressed with our new constable."

"And the money you raised for Captain Bright's bail will go to the relief fund?" Garrett said, with Susan right behind him and young Davie standing proudly at his side.

"Yes, it will. And just in time."

When Breezy left, Garrett and the others finished their dessert.

"Well," Uncle Wilbur said to Garrett, "you've had quite a first two weeks in our sleepy little village, haven't you?"

"You can say that again."

"We don't have murders every day of the week," Susan said. "Thank God."

"But plenty of prowlers, it seems," Uncle Wilbur said with a wink.

"Plenty of lonely ladies, you mean," Garrett said.

And they all laughed.

# ABOUT THE AUTHOR

DON GUTTERIDGE is the author of fifty books: fiction, poetry and scholarly works. He was born in Sarnia and raised in the nearby village of Point Edward. He graduated from Western University in Honours English and taught there for twenty-five years in the Faculty of Education. He is currently Professor Emeritus and lives in London Ontario.

CPSIA information can be obtained
at www.ICGtesting.com
Printed in the USA
LVOW12s2028010916

502845LV00004B/206/P